SHERLOCK HOLMES
MYSTERY MAGAZINE

VOLUME 3, NUMBER 1   SPRING 2012

SO-AFN-787

FEATURES

FICTION

CLASSIC REPRINT

ART & CARTOONS

"I THINK WE'RE DEFINITELY IN THE WRONG NOVEL, WATSON."

CORRECTION

Last issue, we credited the wrong cover artist. The cover was actually by Rhys Davies. We are reprinting it on the back cover with proper credit. (Sorry, Rhys!)

Publisher: John Betancourt | Editor: Marvin Kaye

Sherlock Holmes Mystery Magazine is published by Wildside Press, LLC. Single copies: $10.00 + postage. U.S. subscriptions: $39.95 (postage paid) for the next 4 issues in the U.S.A., from: Wildside Press LLC, Subscription Dept. 9710 Traville Gateway Dr., #234; Rockville MD 20850. International subscriptions: see our web site at www.wildsidemagazines.com. Available as an ebook through all major ebook etailers, or our web site, www.wildsidemagazines.com.

FROM WATSON'S SCRAPBOOK

Mrs Hudson is still in Yorkshire nursing her mother's ailing sister Ruth, but though she is unable to contribute her customary column to this issue of *Sherlock Holmes Mystery Magazine,* she did manage to talk on the telephone with C E Lawrence, whose latest suspense thriller *Silent Victim* was excerpted in our last issue. (C E, by the way, is the pen name of our ongoing contributor, Carole Buggé). I am pleased that Mrs Hudson found the time to send us a record of their conversation.

I am less pleased, however, about what I am about to tell you. You see, in our preceding issue, I persuaded (retired) Inspector Lestrade to send us a few of his recollections, in lieu of Mrs Hudson's usual column. In this regard, my co-editor Mr Kaye made contact with Holmes's ongoing nemesis Professor James Moriarty, and, to my surprise and dismay, actually persuaded him to contribute a column of his own. And unlike Lestrade, who was flattered to be asked, the Professor naturally insisted on being paid! I shudder to think what use our funds may be put to!

In this number of *Sherlock Holmes Mystery Magazine,* Holmes and I appear in two different adventures. The first one is my own reportage of *A Scandal in Bohemia.* I pray that anyone who reads it here for the first time will pay attention to what I have actually written concerning Holmes and affairs of the heart. So far as I know, he never harboured feelings that could in any fashion be construed as romantic in the emotional sense of that word, and that does include *the* Woman—although I do admit there is a mystery that I have never fathomed concerning that stout consulting detective based in New York City.

To my astonishment, the other Holmesian narrative in this issue, *The Dead House,* was written up by none other than Holmes himself!

And now it is time to hear from my co-editor Mr Kaye.

—John H Watson, MD

⚹ ⚹ ⚹ ⚹

One might well call this our "retro" issue of *Sherlock Holmes Mystery Magazine.* Normally, we like to balance our mix with adventures from days bygone and modern, but most of the tales in this seventh issue of *SHMM,* are set in earlier times. The only comparatively recent story is Janice Law's *The Double,* but even it depends partly on earlier Russian Communist history. Marc Bilgrey's *A House Divided* tells an American Civil War incident, while both David Ellis's *A Letter from Legrand* and Michael Mallory's *The Premature Murder* take place in Nineteenth Century America.

Edgar Allan Poe is central to the latter pair of stories. *A Letter from Legrand* is an ingenious sequel to Poe's classic *The Gold-Bug.* While it is not necessary to know the original story, I believe a reacquaintance with it will enhance reading enjoyment of Mr. Ellis's sequel. *The Premature Murder,* though fiction, is a striking investigation into the mysterious death of Edgar Allan Poe in 1849 in Baltimore.

Next issue will feature a far-flung assortment of authors—an amusing tale of a stolen baseball bat by Jeff Baker, of Wichita Kansas; a new Kelly Locke story from Hal Charles in Kentucky; a delightful Sherlock Holmes pastiche by Christian Endres, of Germany; a horrifying semi-science fictional murder story by Ben Godby, of Ottowa; a clever SF pastiche of Sherlock Holmes, and an upsetting story of wrongful death (which the author says really happened) by Stefanie Stolinsky, of Los Angeles.

See you soon!

Canonically yours,
Marvin Kaye

MORIARTY'S MAILBAG

When I, Professor James Moriarty, was approached by the editor of this magazine, and asked if I would contribute an advice column for the present issue, I was, to say the least, surprised. Foremost, I wondered, how this editor find me? The world's greatest detective, Sherlock Holmes, has been searching for me for years, without the slightest success. So, for that matter, has Scotland Yard. Yet, now, a mere editor of a second rate penny dreadful, takes it upon himself one afternoon, to make a few preliminary inquiries, and suddenly, within minutes, manages to discover my ultra secret inner sanctum sanctorum. I am not some petty pick pocket who lives in a run-down flophouse in White Chapel, I am the most powerful criminal mastermind on earth. (Though, I must say, I do occasionally enjoy a nice stroll in the White Chapel district, but that is neither here nor there.)

In addition I am repulsed by the decision to name this publication, *Sherlock Holmes Mystery Magazine,* after my arch enemy, and sworn nemesis. (Not to mention despised rival.) What resident lunatic at the Bedlam Asylum thought this was a sensible idea? A far more appropriate name for a quality periodical, would be, *Professor James Moriarty's Mystery Magazine.* I suggest the publishers consider making this change as soon as possible.

All of which brings me back to the self-same editor of this little pulp digest. What could possibly have possessed this ink drenched renegade from Grubb Street to make him believe that I, the greatest villain who ever lived, would even be interested in answering questions about my criminal methods for the general public? After all, I have a vast crime network to oversee. Does this editor really think I have the time to waste in the petty pursuit of his frivolous and misguided enterprise?

But as it happens, I must admit that I was intrigued by the sheer audacity that this man displayed in seeking me out, and upon further reflection, I now find my interest somewhat piqued . . . as a result, I have decided to temporarily set aside my disdain for the entire human race long enough to participate in this exercise in futility and respond to some missives from the general populous.

[Editorial note—I fear the Professor has underestimated my friend Holmes, for it was he who informed Mr Kaye of the address of Moriarty's eyrie, so to speak.—JHW]

✗ ✗ ✗ ✗

Dear Professor Moriarty,

I have recently embezzled a sizable suym from my employers at a large, and well respected bank. What shall I do with the money?

—Loaded in Lancashire

Dear Loaded,

Place it all in a bag, and send it to me.

✗ ✗ ✗ ✗

Professor Moriarty,

I have an excellent plan for an extortion plot involving a number of prominent citizens. How can I avoid being caught?

—Confident In Cornwall

Dear Confident,

To begin with, I would suggest that you don't send letters to people you don't know, boasting about crimes you haven't yet committed.

✗ ✗ ✗ ✗

Dear Professor Moriarty,

I am an inmate at Newgate Callendar prison. I would like to escape. Can you help me?

—Your friend, 248072931

Dear 248072931,

Enclosed is a file and a recipe for a cake that you can bake the file into.

✗ ✗ ✗ ✗

Dear Professor Moriarty,

I'm an artist who is planning to counterfeit fifty pound notes. Your thoughts would be appreciated.

—Baffled in Blackpool

Dear Baffled,
   When you draw Her Royal Majesty, Queen Victoria, make sure she isn't winking, or in her knickers.

✗   ✗   ✗   ✗

Dear Professor Moriarty,
   My husband is having an affair with my best friend. I plan on poisoning the both of them. What kind of poison would you recommend I use?
—Beth in Bath

Dear Beth,
   I'm very sorry, madam, but I simply cannot condone a crime that is committed for any reason other than profit.

✗   ✗   ✗   ✗

Dear Professor Moriarty,
   Why are you called the Napoleon of crime? Since the English defeated Napoleon, why aren't you called the Wellington of crime?
—Concerned in Kensington

Dear Concerned,
   You sir, are an idiot.

✗   ✗   ✗   ✗

Dear Professor Moriarty,
   Is it true that you control all the crime in London?
—Wondering in the West End

Dear Wondering,
   Yes, it's true. If a school boy steals a loaf of bread from a bakery, I get half.

✗   ✗   ✗   ✗

Dear Professor Moriarty,
   What is the best way to rob a bank and not get caught?
—Befuddled in Brighton

Dear Befuddled,
   Subcontract.

✗ ✗ ✗ ✗

Dear Professor Moriarty,
    What is your opinion of Sherlock Holmes?

—Curious in Cardiff

Dear Curious,
    I think he's a fat, bloated, pompous, know it all. No, wait, that's his brother, Mycroft. Sherlock is all right, though he does tend to go off on those silly tangents of his about cigar ashes, different kinds of mud, boot marks , and the like. Oh, let's face it, the man is a crashing bore.

✗ ✗ ✗ ✗

Dear Professor Moriarty,
    How is it that you did not die when you fell into the Reichenbach Falls with Sherlock Holmes?

—Pondering in Picadilly

Dear Pondering,
    That's simple. It wasn't me who fought Holmes that day, it was a look-a-like actor that I hired to play me. And, in an odd twist of fate, apparently Holmes had done the same. Sadly, both actors drowned. While they were locked in mortal battle, Holmes and I were having cocktails in Davos. Afterwards, we went to our banks in Zurich, and visited our money.

✗ ✗ ✗ ✗

Dear Professor Moriarty,
    How have you managed to elude capture for all these years?

—Reluctant in Regent Park

Dear Reluctant.
    I own a very, very well oiled bicycle.

✗ ✗ ✗ ✗

Dear Professor Moriarty,
    How can I get my boyfriend of five years to propose to me?

—Betty in Billingsgate

Dear Betty,

You must have me confused with Miss Katherine, the agony columnist, for the Daily Mail.

✗

COMING NEXT TIME . . .

STORIES! ARTICLES!
SHERLOCK HOLMES & DR. WATSON!

Sherlock Holmes Mystery Magazine #8 is just a few months away!

Not a subscriber yet? Send $39.95 for 4 issues (postage paid in the U.S.) to:

Wildside Press LLC
Attn: Subscription Dept.
9710 Traville Gateway Dr. #234
Rockville MD 20850

You can also subscribe online at www.wildsidemagazines.com

SCREEN OF THE CRIME

THE ADVENTURES OF THE SIX NAPOLEONS... OF CRIME

by Lenny Picker

Whatever else *Sherlock Holmes: Game of Shadows* does, it deserves credit for enabling a return to movie prominence of one of the all-time great villains and, arguably, the third most interesting Canonical character, who makes a strong impression all out of proportion to his very limited time on-screen. Watson, our trusted eyes and ears, only sees him twice, but his impact on the Good Doctor's life could hardly have been greater. I refer, of course, to Professor James Moriarty, the *ne plus ultra* of arch-enemies, a genius who is "the organizer of half that is evil and of nearly all that is undetected" in the London of 1891. But as intriguing a character as Moriarty is, filmmakers using him as the main bad guy have almost always had to depart from one of the most remarkable aspects of his criminality.

It's always best to return to fundamentals, so let's revisit Holmes's (apparently)[1] first description of his intellectual equal in "The Final Problem."

---

1   Squaring Watson's reaction to Holmes' account of Moriarty in "The Final Problem," with his familiarity with the criminal in *The Valley of Fear*, has challenged Sherlockians for almost a century.

He is a genius, a philosopher, an abstract thinker. He has a brain of the first order. He sits motionless, like a spider in the center of its web, but that web has a thousand radiations, and he knows well every quiver of each of them. He does little himself. He only plans. But his agents are numerous and splendidly organized. Is there a crime to be done, a paper to be abstracted, we will say, a house to be rifled, a man to be removed—the word is passed to the Professor, the matter is organized and carried out. The agent may be caught. In that case money is found for his bail or his defence. But the central power which uses the agent is never caught—never so much as suspected.

That passage tells us why it is if not actually impossible, it's highly improbable for the writers of TV or movie pastiches to stay faithful to one of his most unique qualities. Remember: "He sits motionless," "He does little himself. He only plans." Taken at face value, Moriarty is not, as he's popularly labeled, Holmes's evil twin. His armchair malevolence is really the mirror-image of the Canon's great sedentary collection of grey cells, and the inspiration for Nero Wolfe, Mycroft Holmes. But it would take an extremely gifted writer to make an armchair vs. armchair battle of wits gripping, and even such an author would find translating such words on the page (or e-reader screen) to dialogue and moving images daunting.

Similarly, Moriarty's immobile inhabiting of the center of his web is also nearly-impossible for a pastiche. The Canonical Moriarty has multiple layers insulating him from culpability—a concept brilliantly realized in Bert Coules's flawless adaptation of "The Final Problem" for radio—where Holmes compares the Moriarty organization to a pyramid, with the Professor at the apex, who has dealings only with the nine members of his High Table. But having the main bad guy only seen issuing orders to his minions isn't a recipe for dramatic conflict. All of which is to say that it would be a tough sell for studios and audiences alike to have a Moriarty who just sits and thinks at the center of his gang.

If the frenetic previews of *Game of Shadows*, which contain action sequences similar to those in the first film, are a reliable barometer, they suggest that Jared Harris's Professor will be mixing it up physically with Downey's energetic detective.

But if the latest Moriarty ends up striking viewers as less-than-Canonical (hopefully a judgment that takes into account all of his scenes, not just the presumed fight ones), there is ample precedent for a movie Napoleon of Crime who is active in the field, which, I contend, is a necessary departure from the Canon. In the interests of presenting depth rather than breadth, (and justifying this column's intended-to-be-clever title), I will look at only six predecessors to Harris in essaying the role. Limiting coverage to film and TV portrayals excludes two of the most memorable ones—Orson Welles, in the Gielgud/Richardson radio series of the 1950s, and Michael Pennington, in the standout Merrison/Williams complete audio Canon of the 1990s—but the scripts they benefitted from adhere closely to the language of "The Final Problem." That advantage would make comparing them to the film versions like comparing apple pips to orange pips.

Basil Rathbone's first of three different Moriartys, George Zucco in 1939's *The Adventures of Sherlock Holmes*, remains one of my personal favorites, and not just because the film was the first Holmes one I'd seen.

The epigraph sets the stage for a movie where the Holmes-Moriarty duel is front and center. The viewer is treated to an excerpt of Holmes's journal, while a haunting tune, that would later prove a key to a murder mystery, plays in the background: "In all my life I have encountered only one man whom I can truthfully call the very Genius of Evil—Professor Moriarty. For eleven years he has eluded me. All the rest who have opposed him are dead. He is the most dangerous criminal England has ever known."

(In yet another inexplicable, unnecessary departure from Canon—albeit less egregious than tampering with the dog in the nighttime classic line in the Christopher Plummer *Silver Blaze*—the signed entry is dated 1894, three years after the Reichenbach duel of the Canon.)

This opening spells out explicitly the immensity of the challenge before Holmes, who has tried to bring the professor to book for over a decade[2], a reasonable extrapolation from the Final Problem's duration of the battle—"For years I have endeavored to break through the veil which shrouded it." And the first scene

---

2   And in a more restrained manner than the movie ads—"The Struggle of Super-Minds in the Crime of the Century!"

gets right to it—we see a bearded and bespectacled Moriarty in the dock for murder, acquitted moments before Holmes rushes in too late to present his proof that the crucial alibi—giving a lecture before numerous members of the Royal Society, is a fabrication. (Sherlockian film historians have revealed that the explanation for how such an alibi could have been faked was included in the original script, but this is a case where speculating about how Moriarty pulled it off is better than reading what the writers actually came up with.)

We should stop here to note that the Canonical Moriarty would seem to never need an alibi—he's a planner, not an executioner, or as T.S. Eliot put it in "Macavity, the Mystery Cat," "And whatever time the deed took place—MACAVITY WASN'T THERE!" He wouldn't get his hands bloody—one of the unresolved issues for me from the Canon is why the Professor, who is not a physically imposing man, and who knew of Holmes's self-defense prowess, resorted to hand to hand combat, when some remnants of his organization who had escaped the net could have been utilized.

But what Edwin Blum and William Drake's screenplay—billed as based on Gillette's play, but apart from naming one of the Professor's henchman Bassick, resemblances are relatively few—demonstrates is that even such a departure can work when the spirit of the confrontation is preserved. And the scene where a freed Moriarty offers Holmes a cab-ride back to Baker Street is one of the high points of all Sherlockian cinema. Listen to Rathbone's Holmes: "You've a magnificent brain, Moriarty. I admire it. I admire it so much I'd like to present it pickled in alcohol to the London Medical Society." Some of the dialogue is lifted straight from "The Final Problem"'s Baker Street encounter. The writers cleverly make Moriarty echo Holmes's sentiments from "The Final Problem"—during their cab ride together, Moriarty says that "once [he's] beaten and ruined [Holmes], I'll retire," reinforcing the notion that the two men are two sides of the same coin[3]. Moriarty also displays his hubristic scheming brilliance by telling his adversary that he will "pull off the most incredible crime of the

---

3   Along the same lines, the script has Moriarty deduce from the presence of a spider's web on a watering can that his servant has lied to him.

century," right under Holmes's nose, a boast that he comes very close to realizing.

That sophisticated, layered plot does have Moriarty as a hands-on criminal, but what choice did Drake and Blum have? To dilute the power of the struggle by introducing an interesting wearer of criminal boots on the ground would lessen the impact of the conflict. Zucco is widely considered one of the best-ever Moriartys, capable of conveying menace with just a subtle facial expression or slight change in intonation, an appraisal that makes up for the ignominy of the actor's being billed after the boy playing Billy the Page.

The shift of the Rathbone/Bruce series to a contemporary setting put an extra burden on the writers of movies with Moriarty as the villain. *Sherlock Holmes and the Secret Weapon* (1943) has Moriarty working with the Nazis, and personally participating in the attempted abduction of an Allied scientist. Lionel Atwill, who was a nicely-creepy Dr. Mortimer in the 1939 Hound, has much less to work with than Zucco, and isn't given an interesting crime to plan. If his character was renamed Lysander Starr, not much would be different. Substitute Atwill for Zucco in The Adventures, and his portrayal would be more highly regarded.

Henry Daniell (Rathbone's personal favorite Moriarty, by the way) fares somewhat better in *The Woman In Green* (1945). A desperate Scotland Yard turns to Holmes to solve the Finger murders, apparently-random atrocities that reawaken fears from the Ripper's autumn of terror. In a variation of the pretext the Canonical professor used to get Watson out of the way in Meiringen, Daniell's Moriarty has the doctor lured away with a bogus claim of a medical emergency.

Once he's done so, he and Holmes have a genteel verbal sparring match, with memorable dialogue lifted straight from "The Final Problem"—

"All that I have to say has already crossed your mind."

"Then possibly my answer has crossed yours."

This Moriarty uses more human pawns to achieve his ends than Atwill's, but that fidelity to the organizational model of the Canon means that there are fewer scenes of Holmes and Moriarty together than would be ideal. He does expose his liberty and his life by not remaining at a safe remove at the climax even without the (apparent) necessity the Canonical Professor had because his organization is in tatters. As with Atwill, Daniell is hampered by the script.

A discussion of the next big-screen Moriarty—Hans Sonker's Professor in 1962's *Sherlock Holmes and the Deadly Necklace*— must wait a future column on Worst Sherlock Holmes Films Ever, one which, as editor Marvin Kaye has convinced me, the world is not yet prepared for.[4] And while Laurence Olivier, from 1976's *The Seven Percent Solution*, is the most noteworthy actor to play Moriarty on screen, Nicholas Meyer's revisionist take on the character makes discussion of the character's criminality moot.

So, we'll jump ahead to 1988, the next time the Professor was in a movie—the unsuccessful farce, *Without A Clue*. The usually-excellent Paul Freeman, still best-known for his René Belloq in *Raiders of the Lost Ark*, is in the same boat as Olivier to some extent. His character is merely a plot device in a movie where murder is played for laughs. In contrast to Zucco's Moriarty, who's present from the get-go, Freeman's Moriarty doesn't appear until a quarter of the movie has passed. His character gets his hands bloody, and delegates only the most menial chores to his unprepossessing henchmen. This places him in the vulnerable center of the action when the authorities close in on a counterfeiting operation. And it's hard to imagine the author of *The Dynamics of an Asteroid* ending up in the same fix as does Freeman's character at the end.

The short-lived, promising, if flawed, Ian Richardson series of television films fell victim to the popularity of Jeremy Brett, but at the outset, Ian McKellen was mentioned as a possible Moriarty. The original concept for an incorporation of the Napoleon of Crime into the series led to one of the most offbeat, ostensibly, straight portrayals—that of Anthony Andrews in 1990's TV film, *Hand of a Murderer* (also released as *The Napoleon of Crime*), written by Charles Edward Pogue, screenwriter for Richardson's *Hound of the Baskervilles* and *The Sign of Four*. The movie opens in 1900, with Edward "The Equalizer" Woodward's Holmes outdoing Rathbone's. He's not only gotten Moriarty convicted of murder, but has helped the Professor end up on the gallows (while

---

4   I don't remember discouraging Lenny from writing such a column, but I have a poor memory. At any rate, I will certainly welcome such a column, should Lenny decide to write it for us.—MK

apparently leaving the Professor's organization unscathed.) But Holmes isn't seen before Moriarty, which is what I believe to be a first. Of course, for the story to continue, the execution doesn't come off, as the result of several contrivances, including Holmes's absence, and Scotland Yard's understaffing. Lestrade shuts the barn door after the Professor has fled, setting 300 officers on his trail, though they would have been better-deployed at the gallows.

The script's failings need not all be enumerated here, but Andrews, whose character is given a love-interest, plays the Professor as a smug, mugging-for-the-camera Victorian Joker as interpreted by Jack Nicholson a year earlier, rolling his eyes and chewing the scenery at every opportunity. Pogue does play at least unconscious homage to *The Woman In Green* twice, including a scene where Moriarty's attractive henchwoman mesmerizes someone, and using the same there's-an-ill-patient-in-need-of-help ploy to get Watson out of the way for a recreation of the Baker Street confrontation, here, alas, devoid of any impact or power. Although "The Final Problem" and *The Valley of Fear* do not speak to Moriarty's displays of emotion, there is every reason to believe that in this area, too, he was Holmes's counterpart.

Thus, Andrews's Moriarty's loss of temper during an interrogation is out of character for the Canonical figure; Pogue has his Professor state that "sometimes, rage overwhelms me." Having Moriarty also be a user of cocaine could have been a nice touch if the plot emphasized the ways in which he mirrors Holmes, but in the absence of such emphasis, it's just a throwaway detail, as is the Professor's use of disguise. The ending is as reliant on contrivances as the opening, with the Professor conveniently failing to post guards at his headquarters, an unintended parallel to the unwise police manpower allocation at the gallows.

(DVD-viewing is not this movie's friend, as the ability to freeze an image reveals that a newspaper report of Holmes's death is buried in the middle of an article on Venezuela!)

It is always good to end on an upbeat note, and fortunately, one is provided by the Granada TV series adaptation of "The Final Problem." The script adheres closely to the Canon, and benefits from an addition to the previous aired episode, "The Red-Headed League." That story ends with the revelation that Moriarty was behind John Clay's scheme, providing a nice set-up for what was then considered the series' finale. And the insertion of the Professor into other Canonical stories has a solid basis in the originals. One of the all-time best scholarly essays on the Canon, Robert Pattrick's *Moriarty Was There* (fortunately reprinted in 2011's *The Grand Game* Volume I), ingeniously picks up on the curious incident of a missing letter *s* to deduce Moriarty's hand behind "The Red-Headed League," and "The Five Orange Pips," among others.

The John Hawkesworth script also utilizes the idea first advanced by Edward F. Clark, Jr. in 1963's "Study of an Untold Tale," that Moriarty's attempt to steal the Mona Lisa constituted one of the areas where Holmes foiled Moriarty.

And that script was well-served by the standout cast, including the most-faithful-to-the-Canon Professor in the person of Eric Porter, who mastered the reptilian oscillation Holmes chillingly described to Watson. Visually, Porter is the closest fit yet to Sidney Paget's rendition of the character. And his Baker Street battle of words with Holmes sets a standard that will be hard for future adaptations to match. None of the other five Napoleons of Crime covered here come close to Porter's ability to convincingly portray a criminal mastermind whose wedding of sophisticated organization to villainy made him the adversary for the Great Detective.

The Ritchie films follow the Granada series in one respect: having Moriarty as a shadowy, behind-the-scenes figure in the first film, before putting him front-and-center in *Game of Shadows*, adds menace and significance to the character. The way the Professor is portrayed there will renew the debate about where this series adheres to and departs from the spirit, and the details, of the original.

✗

Lenny Picker, who also reviews and writes for *Publishers Weekly*, founded the Queens scion society, the Napoleons of Crime. Of his work for that society, it can be accurately said that he did little himself. He still hopes to someday read the great Holmes-Moriarty novel that fleshes out their pre-Final Problem duel. He can be reached via his wife's email, <chthompson@jtsa.edu>.

C. E. LAWRENCE

THE DARKER HALF OF CAROLE BUGGÉ

Conducted by (Mrs) Martha Hudson

I regret that for the past two issues, I have been unavailable to write my customary contributions to Sherlock Holmes Mystery Magazine, but thanks to the wonders of modern communications, I have managed to interview another of this magazine's frequent contributors, Miss Carole Buggé. (Forgive me for eschewing the use of 'Ms," which strikes me as an unharmonious neologism.)

Dr Watson, I may say, is quite taken with Carole. After reading her shorter fiction, as well as what I understand are called her three "cosy" Berkley Books mystery novels, *Who Killed Blanche Dubois?, Who Killed Dorian Gray?*, and *Who Killed Mona Lisa?*, the good doctor permitted her access to his notebooks; as a result she has given us two new Sherlock Holmes novels, *The Star of India* and *The Haunting of Torre Abbey*, as well as quite a few shorter Holmesian adventures.

It is rather an open secret, however, that for the past several years, she has taken to writing much darker mysteries, the "Silent" series *y clept*, under the pen name of C E Lawrence: *Silent Screams, Silent Victim*, and the most recent, *Silent Kills*. All of them feature a deeply troubled New York City forensic profiler named Lee Campbell, and in each he must track down truly frightening serial killers.

Below is a transcript of our conversation about her new persona. For convenience, my questions are prefaced by *H* for Hudson, whereas Carole's replies are designated *CE*.

✗   ✗   ✗   ✗

H: What does the C. E. stand for, may I ask?

CE: Carole Elizabeth. Lawrence is a family name.

H: What prompted you to begin a series of books about serial killers?

CE: I've always been interested in hidden behavior, in people's dark sides, perhaps in part because in my family no one was supposed to have a dark side; these things were never talked about, so that made me even more curious about it. Also, I think most writers have a natural interest in psychology, in human behavior, and what can be more intriguing to a writer than extreme behavior? And it seems to me that serial killers are about as extreme as it gets.

H: Is that why you write chapters from the killer's perspective?

CE: Yes. I think it would be very challenging but almost impossible to write a book in which the killer is the protagonist. It was done in American Psycho, of course, but not entirely successfully, I think. So I knew the killer couldn't be the hero, but I wanted to explore his mind in some way, so I came up with idea of having very short chapters from his point of view. I'm not sure if I succeeded, but I wanted to try to get inside the murderer, in Chesterton's famous phrase.

H: Why create a protagonist who suffers from depression? Weren't you afraid that might turn some readers away?

CE: I was actually given advice early on that I should stay away from having a damaged hero, that readers would want a kind of super-hero detective, but in reality I believe that damaged heroes are the only interesting kind (a lot of so-called super-heroes are damaged, after all: Superman is an orphan and an alien on a strange planet, and Batman is a weirdo with a bat fetish). Also, we're all damaged by the time we reach adulthood, some more than others, of course, but I feel that suffering and loss are two of life's constants, and that depression is a very real and understandable reaction to the shock of living, what Shakespeare so memorably called life's slings and arrows. And I think a lot more people suffer or have suffered from various degrees of depression than we probably realize. And, of course, when I wrote the book I had recently been through my own bout of clinical depression.

H: What kind of research did you do for this book?

CE: I have a huge library of forensic books of all kinds, from *Dead Men Do Tell Tales* by Michael Baden to *Forensics of Fingerprints Analysis*. I spent a lot of nights reading and taking notes and, of course, there are some wonderful shows on television, especially *Forensic Files*, which I watch religiously. You can get all kinds of plot ideas from those shows, which are about real crimes and real people. I've been studying forensic psychology for some time through books, and I also took a graduate course at John Jay College for Criminal Justice, taught by Dr. Lewis Schlesinger. He was kind enough to let me audit the class, which was excellent, and also gave me his very informative and scholarly textbook, *Sexual Homicide*, which was one of the textbooks for that class. Interestingly, most of the students were women and I found it interesting that they often sat there calmly eating their lunch as we passed around horrific crime scene photographs. The men in the class seemed more disturbed by it than the women did. The research I did for this book was nowhere near as challenging as the research I did for my physics play *Strings* (for about a year I read physics books nonstop. It was really fun, but after a while, my head was spinning with quarks and muons and neutrinos)!

H: What was the most difficult thing about writing this book?

CE: Plot. Plot, plot, plot . . . did I mention plotting? Or, as Robert McKee would say, story. It was for this book and every other book I've ever written. I think any writer who claims that plots come easily to him/her is either a liar or a fool. It's a bitch and a struggle and that saying about characters writing their own stories is pure nonsense. Oh, you can get away with that in a short story, sure, where you have only one event and one through line. But in a novel, where there are plots and subplots and multiple characters and 400 plus pages to fill with twists and surprises, you bloody well better put your plotting hat on and keep it on until your forehead bleeds, or you're not doing your job. You have to keep coming up with ways to thicken the plot and twist it and turn the story and make it unexpected without making it feel contrived . . . that is never pretty and it's never, ever easy. You know the genre of movie where the hero has cornered the villain in a warehouse, and there are all these barrels around and the bad guy picks one up and throws it at the hero, and he ducks, and the villain throws another one and he jumps over it, and so on? Well, you have to keep throwing barrels at your hero. And then you have to find new ways for him to jump out of the way. Your arms get really tired, and your brain starts to hurt, and you really want to stop, but you have to keep throwing those barrels. You have to make choices that seem original and surprising and yet entirely in keeping with the logic of the story. I care a lot about writing style, and graceful prose, but all the pretty writing in the world won't hide a soft spot in your story.

H: Did you have any "Aha!" moments while working on this particular plot?

CE: Funny you should ask. I did, as a matter of fact. I had two such moments. The first one was after my agent had received a few rejections of the book, and I was getting a sense that though people liked the characters, they weren't sucked in enough by the story. I didn't know how to make it work, but I wasn't ready to give up. At the time I was a summer resident of Byrdcliffe Arts Colony at the time, which is a lovely, idyllic spread of cabins in the woods on a mountainside overlooking Woodstock, New York. They have a kick ass library system in Ulster and Dutchess County, and so I took out *The DaVinci Code* on tape from the Woodstock Library. I had no television, no cable, no VCR, only my tinny little radio and my books on tape. It was, in many ways, the perfect life. I would listen to *The DaVinci Code* while I worked out every night in my cabin. I'm not sure the exact moment it hit me, but it gradually became clear to me there was a powerful lesson to be learned from that book: one thing Dan Brown does so well in it is to keep the pressure up at all times. There is a constant sense of danger and peril to the protagonist, from the first page to the end. I realized that's what was missing from my book, and that there were flaccid scenes and chapters where people sat around comfortably talking philosophy or psychology or whatever. So I took out my cutting knife and whole chapters flew out the window. And I added a stabbing, a shooting, a car chase, a hanging, a beating, and in general just ratcheted up the tension more. And then we sold the book.

H: You said you had two such moments. What was the other one?

CE: That was a real classic "Aha!" moment. It was that same summer at Byrdcliffe, and I had just started out on a jog from my cabin on a beautiful evening in mid-July. I was jogging down Byrdcliffe Road when it hit me all of a sudden: I realized what the book needed was a major twist at the end, and I knew at that moment what the twist had to be. I had been working on this book for two years now, and I hadn't seen it until that very moment. I remember the exact spot on Byrdcliffe Road where I was when it came to me, literally like a bolt out of the blue. But at the same time I realized that it was as though I had set the twist up all along; I really didn't have to change anything in the rest of the book. It was as if my unconscious mind had been setting it up the whole time; once I saw it, it seemed not only logical but actually inevitable. And yet it was invisible to me until that moment. As Geoffrey Rush says in Shakespeare in Love, "It's a mystery."

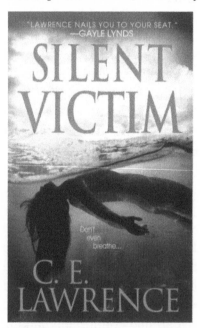 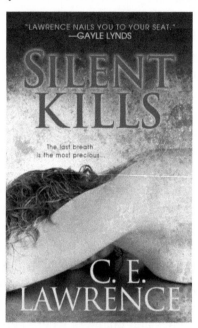

H: Why do you think that is?

CE: Well, my mind was relaxed. The very act of running always jolts something loose in my brain. I would get my best ideas while jogging or mountain climbing or riding my bike up there. Of course, I was engaged all day long in struggling with the problems of writing the book, so my brain was primed, as it were, to come up with solutions, but I was always struck by how those solutions would present themselves at the most unexpected time. In this case, I didn't even know I was looking for a big twist at the end until it popped into my head. But the minute it did, there was no question about it: I recognized the rightness of it.

H: How do you balance being a novelist and playwright? Is it hard moving back and forth?

CE: Actually, I find it refreshing. I feel like some stories are just begging to be plays, while others really need the pages of a novel in order to be properly explored. And then others strike me as screenplays. For instance, I just finished a screenplay about magicians. The title is *The Assistant*.

H: Doesn't each form have its own challenges?

CE: Absolutely. Transition in a screenplay is a whole different technique than transition in a novel, or even a play. But I find it stimulating to move between the different forms. In a novel you have so much space, you can gas on about this and that (within reason, of course), whereas a screenplay is like an epic poem—so condensed, so streamlined. It's story in its most essential form. And you have to think visually, which is great discipline for someone like me. I think one of the greatest dangers to a writer, by definition someone who loves language, is to be drunk with words. Danger, Will Robinson! That can lead to undisciplined, flaccid writing. Screenplay forces you out of that quickly; you're always looking how to condense, condense, condense. And when you're writing a play you have to show everything through dialogue and character interaction. I think it helps you to write better scenes when you're working in prose fiction. You try to make your dialogue character-specific and pithy, just as you would in writing a play.

H: You write music, too, isn't that right?

CE: Yes. I was trained as a classical pianist and singer, and Anthony Moore, my boyfriend at the time, was a composer. (His great uncle was Douglas Moore, the opera composer). Tony had a show done at Yale School of Drama, and he taught me how to do music manuscript so I could help him transcribe songs. One day about a year later I decided to write a musical, a kind of Faustian tale, and I just sat down at my piano and wrote a song. I called him out at his house in Cutchogue and played it for him over the phone. There was this long silence and I thought he hated it, but then he said, "That's really good. It's really interesting." And I knew it was something I could do. I grew up playing the Great Composers, Bach, Beethoven, Brahms, etc., so it never occurred to me until then that was something I could do. I thought they lived on a whole other plane of existence—which was only reinforced by my classical training. I never studied theory or anything like that, but when Tony said he liked my song, I knew it was something I could do. He is a very gifted composer, so I trusted his judgment. And the only thing I enjoy more than writing is writing music. It is an amazingly joyous and completely engaging, sensual thing to do. I've written four complete musicals and am working on a new one, *31 Bond Street*, about a real life murder that took place in the 19th century on Bond Street in New York. It was the O.J. Simpson of its time: a media circus, and was referred to as The Crime of the Century. Jack Finney has written a very good nonfiction book about it called *Forgotten News: The Crime of the Century and Other Lost Stories.*

H: You mentioned Shakespeare a few times. Is there anything special you would like to say about him?

CE: Oh, well, you know, he's the Big Kahuna, isn't he? What can you say . . . the man wrote the most exquisite poetry, dealt with The Big Questions in a way rarely equaled. My only consolation is that he wrote some real stinkers. *The Merry Wives of Windsor* is a wretched, boring play. Thank god.

H: Are there any questions or topics about you, your book, and your life that you would wish to stay away from?

CE: No, my life is an open book. Ha.

✗

SHERLOCK'S BIG FINISH

AN INTERVIEW WITH NICHOLAS BRIGGS

by M J Elliott

There is no doubt that Nicholas Briggs loves the Sherlock Holmes tales. Known around the world as the voice of the Daleks in the phenomenally successful television revival of *Doctor Who*, he also masterminds a range of *Who* audio productions released by the company Big Finish. Briggs writes, directs and performs in many of the dramas (which are available as CDs or downloads from the Big Finish website), appearing alongside the stars of the original series. With 168 *Doctor Who* releases available at the time of writing, you'd think he would have enough on his plate ... but the allure of the adventures of Sherlock Holmes is just too strong.

"I think there are some similarities," Briggs observes, "because the Doctor and Holmes in many ways fulfil the same function in the plots of their respective genres. And quite often, *Doctor Who* stories feel a bit like Sherlock Holmes stories in the sense that some terrible thing has happened and the Doctor comes in to solve the mystery, and, of course, that's what Sherlock Holmes does. I've always seen *Doctor Who* as a kind of mystery thriller, and I think it works brilliantly when it's like that. Quite often, my *Doctor Who* audios follow that mystery thriller format. That is the similarity, and the fact that Holmes is this very singular person, slightly obsessive, with all that information in his brain, and again that's similar to the Doctor."

Big Finish began its association with Holmes when it produced recordings of David Stuart Davies's one-man plays, *Sherlock Holmes—The Last Act* and *The Death and Life of Sherlock Holmes* (the one man in question being actor Roger Llewellyn, who has toured the world with both productions and re-created them in the studio for Big Finish). But for their third audio drama, Briggs took the role of Holmes in a multi-cast production of *Holmes and the Ripper*, another adaptation of a stage play, this one written by Brian Clemens, architect of the Emma Peel era of *The Avengers*. Having already starred in a revival of the production, this was the natural début for the Briggs incarnation of the world's greatest detective, alongside Richard Earl as his faithful Doctor Watson.

In the gap between this series and the next, there followed a dramatisation of one of Conan Doyle's most famous stories, *The Speckled Band*, narrated in large part by Earl (who plays both Watson and the villainous Grimesby Roylott). Briggs explains: "That's what gave me the idea to do *this* series like this—to take out all the 'he said's and 'she said's, but still keep the narration as a very important part. I just wanted to see how that went, and we had a lot of fun with it. I wanted this to feel as authentic as possible, especially in the light of the BBC's new *Sherlock* series (which I really love). But I wanted people who want really proper authentic Sherlock Holmes to have the opportunity to hear dramatised versions. I don't even want to put an extra twist in it, or find a clever way of adapting them. I want, in the case of the Conan Doyle ones, the Conan Doyle voice—I want Watson narrating, I want it to be as authentic as possible." The narration is a very important element for Briggs: "When you've got an audio, you have to find ways of telling the story differently, and if you can't have Watson's voice narrating, you probably have to bend the plot a bit to make things clearer, which is a valid approach. But we don't need to do that, we're being more straightforward. I felt in my gut that was the right thing to do—not by thinking 'What am *I* going to do with Sherlock Holmes?'. Let's give a portal for Sherlock Holmes and Sir Arthur Conan Doyle to speak through. And even with the stuff that isn't Sir Arthur Conan Doyle, we'll still do it in that style."

The second full series of Sherlock Holmes audio dramas by Big Finish begins with Briggs's own adaptation of *The Final Problem* and *The Empty House*, featuring Alan Cox—a former Watson in Barry Levinson's 1985 film *Young Sherlock Holmes*—as Professor Moriarty. I visited the studios during the recording of another Conan Doyle classic, *The Hound of the Baskervilles*. "So many people remember *The Hound of the Baskervilles* because it kind of has a monster in it," Briggs tells me. "And it's a great title, isn't it?" For this production, he has assembled a reliable, highly professional cast he can rely upon to convey the authentic Holmesian atmosphere in a relatively brisk recording session. "I've got together a bunch of actors I know can do it this way, more or less continually recording.

I think Richard Dinnock has done a really good job of adapting it. All the major plot points are there, we all have our little favourite bits, and there are a couple of things that aren't in there. But the plot is all there, and it rockets along." Briggs is no stranger to *The Hound* either, having adapted it for the stage some years earlier, with Samuel Clemens (son of *Holmes and the Ripper* author Brian) as Sir Henry Baskerville, a role he recreates in this audio version. "It was about Watson putting a play on," Briggs recalls, "to which he'd invited Holmes to last rehearsals, and wanted Holmes to play Holmes, to see if it was all authentic. So I brought Holmes back on during the long period when Watson was in Devonshire, and have him ask awkward questions about the plot: 'If you were supposed to be looking after Sir Henry Baskerville, why did you go off to the postmaster?' For the Big Finish production, many of those awkward questions are avoided by the simple act of removing the final explanatory scene in Baker Street. "When you get to the end and the Hound's been killed, and you think, more or less, that Stapleton's gone, and Beryl has been treated so badly and Sir Henry is a mess, it feels fulfilling and that it's the end of the story. You don't miss that explanation in dramatic terms."

But this second series is not made up entirely of Canonical adaptations. Coming in between the Moriarty saga and *The Hound* is *The Reification of Hans Gerber*. "It's an entirely original script that I asked George Mann to do," says Briggs. "George has written lots of stuff for the Black Library, and he's very good at Victorian pastiche. He put himself forward very early on, and suggested a story which I liked, which had an interesting twist. He's written something very much in the style of Conan Doyle, and very much in the style of all of them in this little series—there's a lot of Watson's voice."

Rounding off the second series is a dramatisation of David Stuart Davies's 1992 novel *The Tangled Skein*, which sees the most famous fictional detective of all time battling the most famous vampire, Count Dracula. The adaptation is again by Richard Dinnock, and its placement immediately after *The Hound* is entirely intentional, for *Skein* serves as a semi-sequel to the Conan Doyle classic. It would be unfair to those unfamiliar with Davies's novel to go into further details here—instead, I advise you to purchase them both. Dealing as it does with an undead adversary, we are going further into the realm of the fantastic than usual. Has Briggs ever considered an encounter between Holmes and the Doctor? "I was never tempted to do that, not at all. In *Doctor Who*, everything else we know of as fictional is fictional. So in the world of *Doctor Who*, Sherlock Holmes is fictional. It might be a difficult one. It's not a priority for me to do that."

And what does the future hold for Sherlock Holmes in the very capable hands of Mr Briggs? "I want to see what our audience likes best. I would like to carry on doing a mixture of adaptations and original stuff as well, getting other writers to come up with entirely new Holmes stories which feel like Sir Arthur Conan Doyle." For the time being, though, the masterly first series of adventures can be obtained by visiting www.bigfinish.com.

"Ratchet it down, Hyde."

THE ROOTS OF THE PSYCHIC DETECTIVE IN FICTION

by Lee Weinstein

I

I sat on a stool in the cluttered laboratory beneath my basement apartment. It was chilly enough to make me wear a robe, but the dozen or so candles burning around the room made it look warm. The phone book lay on the table in front of me.

I stared at my ad in the Yellow Pages. It read:

HARRY DRESDEN—WIZARD

Lost items found. Paranormal investigations.
Consulting. Advice. Reasonable Rates.

No Love Potions, Endless Purses,
Parties or Other Entertainment.

This excerpt from a vignette on Jim Butcher's website introduces us to his popular character, Harry Dresden, a hardboiled detective who also happens to be a wizard.

He is the protagonist of a continuing series of novels, *The Dresden Files*, which began in 2000. He is also one of the more recent variations on the psychic or occult detective, a familiar figure in the annals of horror fiction for over a century; a figure that assumes many forms in today's literature. Afficionados of dark fantasy may be familiar with such classical characters as William Hope Hodgson's Carnacki, Algernon Blackwood's John Silence, and Seabury Quinn's Jules de Grandin.

But in recent years, psychic detectives have come in all shapes and sizes from the hardboiled Harry Dresden to TV FBI agents Fox Mulder and Dana Scully of *The X Files* fame to renegade reporter Carl Kolchak. There's the series by Rick Kennett about Ernie Pine, the reluctant ghost hunter (1988-1992), the Charlie Goode stories by Steve Rasnic Tem (1991), the John Taylor character in the

Nightside series, starting in 2003, described by its author, Simon R. Green, as the fantasy equivalent of James Bond, and the female supernatural sleuth, Penelope Pettiweather (1990-1995), by Jessica Amanda Salmonson.

The recent anthology, *Those who Fight Monsters: Tales of Occult Detectives* (2011) edited by Justin Gustainis, contains 14 original stories by writers associated with urban fantasy and paranormal romance, such as Carrie Vaughn, Laura Anne Gilman, and Gustainis himself, an author who has written about the character Quincy Morris, the great grandson of the character in *Dracula*.

But, back before the days of urban fantasy and paranormal romance, the supernatural sleuth has had a long history. This type of character, an investigator who approaches the supernatural using knowledge and logic, has evolved from a familiar model, that of Sherlock Holmes.

Tracing the evolution of this character back through time reveals a number of characters who stand out in the history of this sub-genre. One of the last series before the modern era were the Lucius Leffing stories by Joseph Payne Brennan, which were written in and set in the 1970's but had a distinctly Victorian air about them. Leffing's adventures were chronicled by none other than Joseph Payne Brennan, who cast himself as a character in these stories, as Leffing's Watson figure, a common element to most of these series. Many of them were non-supernatural mysteries, appearing in such places as *Alfred Hitchcock's Mystery Magazine*, but a number involved genuine hauntings of various sorts.

Another series, along slightly different lines, was the Titus Crow series of novels and short stories by Brian Lumley. These appeared from 1970 to 1989. The series was part of the Chthulhu Mythos and Crow was a character who went up against Lovecraftian entities rather than conventional folkloric antagonists.

Manly Wade Wellman's stories about John the Balladeer appeared from the early 60's into the 1980's. John was a backwoods minstrel with a silver-stringed guitar, who wandered through the Appalachians encountering and defeating supernatural menaces. Wellman also wrote a series about John Thunstone, a more traditional type of psychic detective.whose adventures appeared in *Weird Tales* magazine starting in the 1940's. He was a larger-than-life, independently wealthy investigator who sometimes carried a swordcane forged by a saint and dealt with both traditional occult menaces and a few that Wellman had invented for the series such as the humanoid Shonokins.

Also featured in *Weird Tales*, but more well-known, was Seabury Quinn's Jules de Grandin, who appeared in something like 90 stories between 1925 and 1951 and was one of the most popular series to run in *Weird Tales* magazine. Quinn was the magazine's most popular writer. De Grandin was a French physician and expert on the occult who lived in Harrisonville, New Jersey. He was assisted by Dr. Samuel Trowbridge, who acted as his Watson figure. Robert Weinberg notes in the entry for the series in *Survey of Fantasy Literature* (1983) that in these stories Quinn was breaking away from the purely supernatural by incorporating advances in science. Thus in one story a ghost is dissipated by means of a radioactive substance that de Grandin uses as a weapon.

A slightly different sort of occult detective was created by Sax Rohmer (Arthur Sarsfield Ward) of Fu Manchu fame. Morris Klaw was an mysterious elderly-appearing man who solved non-supernatural crimes by psychic means. The stories, which appeared in magazines from 1913 to 1920 were collected as *The Dream Detective* (1920). He would sleep at the scene of the crime on an "odically sterilized" pillow and clues would present themselves in his dreams. (Odic force was a vital force akin to electromagnetism which was hypothesized in the mid-19th century.) Klaw's adventures are narrated by his chronicler, a Mr. Searles, There were originally 9 stories, to which a tenth was added in later editions.

And then there was *The Secrets of Dr. Taverner* (1926) by Dion Fortune (Violet Mary Firth) who was a member of the occultist organization The Order of the Golden Dawn, as was Rohmer. This was a British organization which was extremely influential in occultist belief in the twentieth century. Dr. John Richard Taverner is a psychiatrist and occultist who runs a nursing home, and his cases are narrrated by his Watson, Dr. Eric Rhodes. The cases, were, according to the author, composites based on true occurrances, and Taverner himself was based on Fortune's mentor, a man ironically named Moriarity, William Moriarty. His cases involved possession, vampirism and other occult problems.

Earlier still, and still popular today, were the adventures of Thomas Carnacki chronicled in *Carnacki the Ghost Finder* by

William Hope Hodgson. Six stories appeared from 1910 to 1912 and were published as a book in 1913. In 1947, August Derleth published an expanded version, containing three additional stories, under his Mycroft and Moran imprint.

The Carnacki stories, like much of Hodgson's fiction, anticipated the ideas of H.P.Lovecraft by applying a scientific basis to supernatural events. They also perhaps influenced the Jules de Grandin stories in this sense. Thus Carnacki had to battle entities that came from outside of our normal time and space. He always carried a gun, a camera, and a clever device of his own invention called an electric pentacle. In each story, Carnacki would invite his four friends, Jessop, Arkwright, Taylor, and the viewpoint character, Dodgson, to his home and tell them of his latest adventure. At the end they would question him on various points and he would explain the case, often in terms of a quasi-scientific occult lore of Hodgson's own invention. Thus he speaks of manifestations of such things as aeiirii and saiitii phenomema referred to in a *Necronomicon*-like book called the *Sigsand Manuscript.*

Carnacki is occasionally credited as the being first psychic detective, but he was not. However, Carnacki, of all the psychic detectives, seems to have developed a following in more recent years. There was a BBC adaptation of one of the stories "The Horse of the Invisible" in the 70's starring Donald Pleasance as part of their The Rivals of Sherlock Holmes series; the only supernatural entry. More recently, there have been Carnacki pastiches by other writers. A collection of them by A. F. Kidd and Rick Kennett was published by Ashtree Press: *472 Cheyne Walk—Carnacki: the Untold Stories* (2002) Carnacki also appears as a character in *The League of Extraordinary Gentlemen*. According to John Clute's *Encyclopedia of Fantasy* (1997), the Carnacki stories were published by Eveleigh Nash to fill the niche left when Algernon Blackwood left off writing his John Silence stories. Carnacki's predecessor, *John Silence: Physician Extraordinary* (1908), by Blackwood is also sometimes credited as the first psychic detective. While not the first, he is certainly the first well-known one.

According to S.T. Joshi's introduction to the 1997 edition, the book was given a massive promotion at the time with the slogan "John Silence—the most mysterious character of modern fiction," and became a bestseller.

The book was originally intended to be a collection of five unrelated tales, but Blackwood was requested by the publisher to tie them all together with a single protagonist, The tales involve supernatural problems explained in terms of what today might be called paranormal activity. His stories are generally narrated by his associate, Mr. Hubbard. Blackwood, like Dion Fortune and Sax Rohmer, was a member of the Order of the Golden Dawn.

II

As for the literary roots of the psychic detective, some authors cite Dr, Martin Hesselius, a character created by J. Sheridan Lefanu. as the first such character.

Hesselius was probably inspired by an earlier series of stories by Samuel Warren, that ran in *Blackwood's Magazine* (1831-1837) published in book form as *Passages from the Diary of a Late Physician* (1831). Warren's book is a collection of short stories representing cases of the eponymous and anonymous physician. These stories for the most part do not concentrate on the supernatural and are more concerned with morality than horror. But they are likely the inspiration for Dr. Hesselius who is more of a prototype than an actual occult detective. He appears in the framework of LeFanu's book, *In a Glass Darkly* (1872), to tie together the stories. The conceit is that the stories comprising the volume have been found among his papers after his death. Hesselius appears as a character in only one of the five stories in the collection, which also includes such classic tales as "Carmilla" and "Mr. Justice Harbottle." He appears as a character only in the first story, "Green Tea." in which a clergyman is haunted by a spectral monkey. It should be noted that the clergymen does not seek Hesselius out in his professional capacity as a doctor, They meet informally and Hesselius becomes interested in his case.

Researcher Gary W. Crawford has pointed out the resemblance between that story and the story "The Spectral Dog" in Warren's book. (*LeFanu Studies* 1:1 May 2006) In both stories the protagonist is a clergyman who is haunted by a phantom animal that follows him into a public conveyance. In Warren's story, the dog is supposed to be a hallucination caused by unknown medical reasons, not a supernatural manifestation, whereas LeFanu's monkey is a manifestation of evil.

Other authors have cited Dr. Abraham van Helsing from *Dracula* (1897) as the first psychic detective. Like Hesselius, he is a physician with a knowledge of the occult, and like Hesselius he appears in only one story. He is called in to see Lucy Westerna because he is a physician and she is suffering from a mysterious illness which Dr. Seward cannot cope with alone. He is not called, at least initially, because of his knowledge of the occult.

So neither Hesselius nor Van Helsing are series characters and neither are really detectives.

The appearance of Sherlock Holmes, starting in 1887 in *Beeton's Christmas Annual*, was enormously influential and created a mold for other writers to follow. There were no supernatural elements in any of the stories: Holmes once famously said "No ghosts need apply," but many of the writers who followed in Doyle's footsteps had no such reservations.

L.T. Meade (Elizabeth Thomasina Meade Smith (1854—1914), created two series of Holmes-like detective stories. One series, written in collaboration with Clifford Halifax, *Stories from the Diary of a Doctor* (1894 & 1896) follows the investigations of a physican who deals with unusual cases, and finds natural explanations. The other series was written in collaboration with Robert Eustace, *A Master of Mysteries* (1898), which follows John Bell, another investigator who exposes apparent supernatural cases as hoaxes.

All of these books may be seen as steps toward what we now think of as the psychic detective.

However, the first example of a true psychic detective is Flaxman Low, created by Hesketh and Kate Prichard. Low is not a physician, but an expert on the occult and is the protagonist of a series of stories in which he is requested to investigate hauntings and other supernatural or apparently supernatural manifestations. It is here that a melding occurs between the horror story and the detective story.

Although they represent a pioneering effort, these stories are not as well known as the later series influenced by them such as the John Silence and Carnacki stories. Lovecraft doesn't mention them in his "Supernatural Horror in Literature," and S.T. Joshi doesn't mention them in his introduction to *John Silence*. Low is also not mentioned in *Queen's Quorum: A History of the Detective-Crime Short Story As Revealed by the 100 Most Important Books Published in this Field Since 1845–1951*, although the Prichard's non-supernatural sleuth character, November Joe, is and Thomas Carnacki is incorrectly listed as the first supernatural detective.

Flaxman Low first appeared in a series of six stories in *Pearson's Magazine* in 1898 followed by a second series of six in 1899. Each one ran under the heading "Real Ghost Stories" accompanied by a photograph of the haunted house in question. Each one was titled "The Story of [insert name of home]." All twelve stories were later collected as *Ghosts: The Experiences of Flaxman Low* (1899).

Low is a student of what is termed in the stories "psychology," although today we would call it parapsychology, and he has devoted a good deal of his life to studies of occult phenomena. It could be argued that the authors took the idea of an occult researcher such as Dr. Hesselius and recast it using the Holmes stories as a mold or template. Going L.T. Meade one better, most of these stories are genuinely supernatural.

In the name of verisimilitude, the book is prefaced with an excerpt from a letter, addressed by Low, himself, to the authors in which he explains that he is the first in his field of inquiry to depart from the old conventional methods and to approach supernatural problems along the lines of natural law. He gives them freedom to write about his adventures and asks only that his name be disguised.

Flaxman Low is described as having a high forehead, long neck, and thin mustache.

In the course of his investigations he does more than observe and deduce. On several occasions he risks his life in nearly fatal struggles with supernatural or biological entities

The stories follow a pattern similar to those of Sherlock Holmes. In a typical story, Low is called upon to investigate a haunting. After his arrival he questions his client and listens as the client describes the strange phenomena that have been occurring. Low then proceeds to investigate the matter firsthand and makes his own observations.

Finally he puts the apparently disparate clues together and explains the nature of the haunting. In some stories he solves the case by ending the haunting, and in others, he merely leaves things be. Over the course of the dozen stories, he deals with such occult manifestations as ghosts, vampires, and elementals, finding very unusual and deceptive clues to investigate. Just to keep things interesting, a couple of the stories have non-occult explanations. One involves a deadly form of plant life and another a dangerous form of fungus. One story turns out to be a case of homicide by a murderer with a rare type of poison. In the final two stories he crosses paths with the Moriarity of the series, a Dr. Kalmarkan, an occultist with an evil bent.

There is no Watson character, but that role is often filled by the clients who listen with amazement as Low ties the clues together into a coherent solution.

When the stories originally appeared in *Pearson's Magazine*, they were bylined E. & H. Heron. When they appeared in book form a short time later in 1899 the pseudonyms were dropped and the real names of the authors, Hesketh and Kate Prichard, were credited.

Hesketh Vernon Hesketh-Prichard (1876-1922) was an adventurer, big game hunter, cricketeer, and writer of travel books, among other things. He stood six foot four, or six foot six, depending on which source you consult, but in either case, he was a large man. Among his friends he counted J.M. Barrie and, significantly, Arthur Conan Doyle.

His sometime collaborator, Kate Prichard, was not his wife, but his mother, and according to Jack Adrian, who wrote the introduction to the Ashtree Press edition of *The Experiences of Flaxman Low* (2003), he did most of the writing and Kate added a final polish to the stories.

Hesketh Prichard died at the age of 45 of endocarditis most probably resulting from rheumatic fever.

The Flaxman Low stories were not their most popular or well-known stories by any means. The team's most popular creation was a series of stories and novels about Don Q, an aristocratic and anti-heroic Spanish criminal who specialized in kidnapping.

Hesketh alone wrote the November Joe series, which featured a detective of the backwoods who solved crimes in a Holmesian fashion, but from such clues as would be found in a rustic environment like broken twigs and muddy footprints.

But the stories remain obscure today. For all that they are atmospheric and have imaginative hauntings and clever solutions, Low himself remains a bit of a cipher. He is never really developed as a character. Jack Adrian speculates that the stories did not become well-known for another reason as well—the authors's attempts at verisimilitude may have been too effective, and readers may have mistakenly thought they were actual accounts rather than fictional narratives.

But if not their most popular character, Low may have ultimately been their most influential one.

In the wake of the Low stories, there were imitators, including *The Ghost Hunters* (1905-1906) by Allen Upward and *True Ghost Stories* (1907) by Jessie Adelaide Middleton.

These have fallen into complete obscurity. But the previously mentioned *John Silence: Physician Extraordinary* by Algernon Blackwood has become a classic in the genre. Silence, like Hesselius, is a physician, but like Low and his imitators, is a protagonist who as H.P. Lovecraft put it, "runs a triumphant course" through the series of stories. Like Low, he has a deep knowledge of the occult and has been termed a supernatural Sherlock Holmes.

And it was Low by way of Silence who ultimately paved the way for a genre that is still with us today.

"Coming down kind of hard on shoplifters, aren't you?"

THE DEAD HOUSE

by Bruce Kilstein

My longtime friend, colleague and confidant, Dr John H Watson, has been both my chronicler and steadfast champion in his accounts of my, or I should say *our*, investigations into matters of crime and intrigue. I fear that his versions of events perhaps overstate my abilities and accomplishments to the reading public. I have, however, been remiss in paying him the proper tribute he has ably earned as my assistant. Many are the times that he has proved essential in the successful prosecution of an investigation. I pause here, years later, to relate my dear friend's role in the events concerning Captain Sidney Emmet-Jones.

It was spring of 18__ and Watson and I struggled to fend off the torpor of inactivity brought about by the seasonal rains that confined our bodies to our digs at 221B Baker Street and the lack of any stimulating work to unfetter our minds. Watson made the occasional trip to his surgery to tend to the odd patient while I tried to busy myself in the preparation of a monograph concerning the fascinating new science of fingerprinting. The theory being that the ridges and whorls on the pads of each person's fingers are unique, I set about the task of attempting a system of classification unique to the criminal class. I soon wearied of the painstaking process and turned my attentions from the magnifying lens to the chemistry bench, for the purposes of maintaining a keen edge of observational power, to distill the essence of *Erythroxylon truxillense* in preparation of a seven percent solution.

Watson had just come in from the rain followed by the angry shouts of our housekeeper admonishing him for tracking mud into the vestibule. "No sign of this bloody weather easing up, Holmes," he said.

I grunted little reply, too absorbed in my task.

He approached and began his usual litany of disapproval of my present endeavour. I was spared the lecture and subsequent argument when something at the window diverted my attention.

"Watson," I interrupted, "what do you make of that woman getting out of the coach?"

He approached the window and after a moment's contemplation stated, "Hard to say, Holmes, as she is obscured by the umbrella. I should guess her to be of some advanced age, as she requires the aide of a cane and the assistance of her driver. Other than that, I cannot hazard much else. You, no doubt, would deduce much more from this scene."

"Quite," I replied. "Observe her awkward way of coordinating the use of both umbrella and walking stick, which suggests a recent injury rather than a long term infirmity. Her dress is mourning, which would hint at a recent loss, but note the stylish cut of her robe even in time of bereavement. This is a younger woman of some means as we see that she has the best clothing, servants and a handsome coach and four. Note how her servants are attentive, but she graciously hesitates in accepting their assistance. This would suggest that those in her employ like her. A kind woman, I should think. Moreover she is left-handed as she favours the left for support of the body by the cane, has been feeling weak and eaten little the past few days, evidenced by the pallour of her cheek and slight tremour and hesitancy of her progress. She has, no doubt, suffered some recent shock and visits us for some assistance with a problem. We add the sum of these trifling observations with the obituary section of today's *Times* and we must necessarily conclude that we are about to be visited by the widow of the late Captain Emmet-Jones."

"Astounding, Holmes!" Watson cried as we watched the subject of our deductions exit her ride and make her way to our door. "How do you do it?"

I took pause, relishing the moment of anticipation before some matter of particular challenge and welcomed any chance to dispel the insidious boredom. "Elementary, my dear fellow." I referred Watson to the brief account describing the strange death of Captain Sidney Emmet-Jones in the morning *Times* and rang for my housekeeper. She appeared immediately, apparently already on her way to my rooms to complain about my partner's effluvia in the foyer. I stopped her with a "Yes, of course we will be more careful, Mrs Hudson, but presently we are about to receive a very distraught young widow who deserves our hospitality. Please prepare tea and brandy and show her to our study immediately." With the ring of the doorbell she was off to her task with no more mention of the Doctor's indiscretion.

"What do you make of this, Holmes?" Watson asked, turning from the paper.

"We shall soon learn more details, but I suspect foul doings. We must tread lightly."

Barely had we time to stoke the fire and made a token attempt to make our surroundings presentable, each silently acknowledging Mrs Hudson's observation that we ought to be tidier, when she returned to announce the subject of our speculation.

"Are you Mr Sherlock Holmes?" asked the young lady, rather timidly.

"At your service. Allow me to introduce my colleague, Dr Watson. Watson, Mrs Emmet-Jones."

"How is it you already know my name?" the woman gasped in surprise. "Have we previously made acquaintance?"

"No, my dear, but had we, the pleasure would indeed have been mine. I surmised your identity after reading the account in the morning paper. But you are cold. Won't you take a seat by the warm fire and partake of a refreshment?" Watson helped her to a chair and poured her a restorative draught, which she willingly accepted, while I filled a fresh pipe.

After she had time to settle, I said, "Pray, tell us your concerns. Leave nothing out. You may speak freely before Dr Watson."

"Thank you, Mr Holmes. The police do not seem to be of much help and I have no one else to whom I can turn for advice in this matter. The papers did not tell half the story." She paused and sipped her drink. Staring at the fire, she continued. "I had been wed to my husband just six months after his return from military service in South Africa. He having no relations, we came to live with my father at Dunmore, our family estate in Surrey. At all times he seemed in the most robust of health. He had no immediate complaints of illness in the time just prior to the day we found him on the floor of his study. As you can imagine, we were all quite shocked. Hardly had we time to grasp the sudden gravity of the situation, when the Doctor arrived and pronounced the situation contagious and ordered an immediate internment. Something about a fever brought from Africa. We were naturally confused, but of course agreed."

"Who is the attending physician to your family?" Watson asked.

"Dr Sheridan, but …"

"Charles Sheridan," Watson interjected. "Good man. Top notch. But surely he would have requested an autopsy in so sudden a death in a young man."

"I believe you were about to add something, Mrs Emmet-Jones," I stated.

"Yes. While Doctor Sheridan has been our physician for many years, it was Dr Knox who made the pronouncement and ordered the swift burial."

"And where did this Knox come from?"

"He was a friend of my husband's from the service. He must have been on his way to visit because he appeared before we had time to send for Dr Sheridan." She then lost composure and it took us several minutes and a bit more of the brandied tea until she was able to continue.

Once she had gathered strength I asked, "Clearly the misadventure did not end with the funeral?"

"No. It was after that the real horror began. At Sidney's funeral my father had occasion to discuss events with Dr Sheridan."

"Good man," Watson reiterated.

"So," I continued, referring to the account in the paper, "it was Dr Sheridan who ordered the body, and excuse my lack of a better word, exhumed?"

"Yes, that is correct. The process took several days, what with the legal paperwork required. Some days later, we were obliged to assemble again at the graveside to relive the ordeal. A smaller group this time. Just my father, Dr Sheridan and the inspector from Scotland Yard."

"Was this Dr Knox not in attendance?" Watson inquired.

"No, Doctor. He could not be located. Sidney never left his address and no residence or address of his surgery could be found. Perhaps he had not time to set one up since his return from South Africa."

I paced the room, anticipating what was to come next. "And what did you find upon opening the grave?"

"Nothing, sir," she replied quietly. "Sidney was gone."

The blood ran from Watson's face. Aghast, all he could do was echo the word, "Gone."

"Yes. He was apparently the victim of grave robbers. The inspector said that this happens, not infrequently, to graves of the Upper Classes. Robbers looking for booty buried with the deceased. He said that with no body and no evidence, there was nothing left to investigate. There were no clues."

"Grave robbing, indeed," I said. 'You no doubt fainted at the revelation from the grave and sustained an injury to your ankle. The inspector's name would not have been Lestrade?"

"Why, yes on both counts, Mr Holmes. You astonish me."

"We are well acquainted with the inspector's credentials," I let slip with a measure of sarcastic contempt. "No clues? Why your story today is nothing if not a cornucopia of clues." I helped her from her chair and again rang for Mrs Hudson and escorted her to the door. "Do not fret. I feel we will be able to shed some light on this dark business. We should like to pay you and your father a visit at Dunmore and have a look about. We should also wish to visit the gravesite."

"I would be most grateful to you both. I shall make the arrangements for your arrival."

After she had been escorted from our rooms by Mrs Hudson and we were sure she was out of earshot, I asked, "Well, Watson, what do you make of it?"

"Dastardly, Holmes. Grave robbers? In these modern times? But what can we do? The body has been snatched."

"Maybe. I fear, however, that there may be more to this story than a simple robbery. I ask you, would mere ruffians, intent on gaining some quick profit from the spoils of a newly interred occupant, take the time to replace the dirt from the disturbed grave and leave the site tidy enough so as to avoid the arousal of suspicion until the grave was re-opened by the authorities?"

"I hadn't thought of that, Holmes."

"No, this was no mere crime of opportunity. This goes deeper and speaks of some motive more sinister. Gather your kit for traveling, Watson. Some sturdy boots and slicker, a torch and a stiff walking staff. Your revolver, too, I should think." He stared at me for a moment while I consulted my Beekman's timetable to check on the next train from Waterloo station to Surrey. I took a final draw on my pipe and through the smoke I confirmed his suspicion, "Yes, Watson, the game is afoot."

I remained silent for most of the trip to Dunmore. I smoked quietly and watched the damp countryside pass by as I contemplated the facts of the case. Watson, having worked long enough at my side by then, knew to keep his council at such times, respecting the need for introspection. As we had booked the last private car from Waterloo Station, he passed the time cleaning his service revolver, which had not seen action in some time. We arrived at our destination southwest of the city, in the late afternoon. Lord Hemming, the father of the widow Emmet-Jones, had sent his coach ahead to convey us to Dunmore.

Phelps, his butler, received us at the hall. "Mr Holmes, Dr Watson," he said. "Lord Hemming is expecting you and requests your presence to tea in the study." He took our overcoats and escorted us through the lavish estate.

"Phelps," I asked, "could I trouble you to arrange an interview with the servant who discovered Captain Emmet-Jones's body?"

"It would be no trouble, sir. However, the young woman is no longer in our employ."

"I suspected as much. Have you any idea where she may be found?"

"I do not. Nelly was a young Irish girl who was personally selected by the Captain upon his arrival. He had not taken a manservant as yet. The shock of discovery of the body was apparently too much for the woman and she fled the same day. I must say that she did not seem very well suited to her duties."

"Perhaps not. Would you say she was a comely woman?"

The question seemed to startle Phelps and it was clear that he had not considered the matter before. "Well, yes, she would have been considered quite attractive."

"Thank you, Phelps. You may escort us to his Lordship now."

We soon made the acquaintance of Lord Hemming, a jovial yet stately gentleman. Hemming was seated to tea laid out on a table in the corner of a cluttered room, even by our Baker Street standards. This seemed odd for such a large house, but as we were seated he explained. "Forgive the surroundings, gentlemen, but I thought it best not to waste time, therefore I had tea set in Captain Emmet-Jones's study so that you could immediately begin your investigations. My daughter begs pardon as she was quite exhausted from her journey and recent events and repaired directly to her rooms for repose."

"Very perceptive, your Lordship." I instantly admired his candour and preparation. Watson took a small notebook from his vest and recorded various points of our interview with notes of the surroundings. I fear he also recorded more than a bit of jam from the scones he seemed to enjoy as well. "It would seem that the Captain had yet to unpack all of his belongings."

"Yes, this is so," Hemming replied. "In fact, he insisted on almost absolute privacy in the task. He took many meals here. He hired a servant for assistance and took no visitors here other than his friend, Dr Knox."

"You would therefore not know if any items were missing."

"Correct. The maid, I am afraid, has also taken her leave."

"So we are told," Watson added, balancing his teacup, notebook and the pastry.

After the polite repast we commenced inspection of the room. I made my way carefully about the place and settled near an area in front of a great oak desk. I knelt to inspect the area with my glass. "I take it, owing to this discolouration on the rug, which appears to be of recent origin, that the body was discovered here."

"Yes it was, Mr Holmes," Hemming affirmed.

"Note the fading in the pattern, Watson. Join me if you please." With effort, owing to his wound suffered in India, Watson made his way down to the carpet. "What else do you notice?"

"Well," he replied, "a stain of some sort but certainly not blood. Some caustic agent or solvent, I should think."

"Excellent, my good man." The snack clearly had sharpened his powers of observation. "Do you note the peculiar odour?"

I hid my amusement as I was reminded of a walrus in the zoological gardens, as my friend lay prostrate on the rug with his whiskers hovering just above the nap, while he repeatedly sniffed the area in question. "Quite distinct. Unpleasant, yet somehow familiar."

I produced a small scissors and gestured for permission from Lord Hemming. He nodded his assent and I took a sample of the weave, brushing the clippings into an envelope. I assisted Watson to his feet and turned attention to examination of the desk. All drawers were curiously empty except a bottom drawer, which was locked. As there was no one able to produce a key and the oak was thick, I asked Watson to draw his revolver. "Would you do the honours, Doctor?" We covered our ears, yet the rapport from the weapon shattered not only the lock, but also the silence of the sedate home. This sent servants scrambling to the room, no doubt in anticipation of some further tragedy. We assured Phelps that all was under control and he ushered the throng from the room.

The contents of the drawer were few. An envelope addressed to Emmet-Jones in a female hand, the missive having been removed, a small photograph, as one might place in a locket, along with a ledger book. Inspection of the book revealed a recent deposit of account for a rather large sum drawn at Goslings & Sharp, Fleet Street. I showed the balance to Watson, who raised an eyebrow acknowledging the substantial sum.

"Lord Hemming," I asked, "do you know these bankers?"

"Of course. They have been managing my accounts for years."

"I take it, and by no means do I wish to intrude on your privacy, that Captain Emmet-Jones's recent deposit of this large sum was the result of your personal generosity?"

"Quite so. The man had little means and, I admit, was not the sort I would have selected for my daughter. She did, however, profess a deep love for the chap, and since I would be alone had she married a man of more means, I confess I welcomed the prospect of keeping her here, in my company, with the wish of one day having grandchildren about. I made the bequest so that the Captain should have the capital to start a business venture of his choosing."

"I understand. I fear that we are losing daylight and Watson and I would like to inspect the Captain's gravesite. We have taken too much of your time."

"Nonsense. If there is anything I can do to provide further assistance, I am at your disposal," the gentleman kindly offered.

"There is one thing for now. I would kindly ask you to contact your agents at Goslings & Sharp. Ask them to quote you the current balance of the account we have just discussed." He heartily agreed and I gave him my card as Phelps returned with our accoutrements. "Come, Watson, we have business at Brookwood."

✗ ✗ ✗ ✗

With darkness descending, we made our way to Brookwood Cemetery in Woking. I instructed the driver to wait, as the prospect of finding a cab later in this lonely corner of the city seemed slim. Watson lit his torch as we made our way to the caretaker's house near the main gate. I rapped with my cane repeatedly until the untidy little man answered. When we told him our business, he seemed not to have been forewarned of our arrival and in no way hid his displeasure at being interrupted at his evening meal. With the invocation of Lord Hemming's name as well as the proffering of a half-crown for his trouble, he seemed to regain his memory and summoned a measure of enthusiasm for our enterprise.

We lit additional lanterns and made our way through the maze of memorials, some simple, others ornate sculptures honouring the dead. The wings of marbled angels cast long shadows on the winding path. The gloom, combined with the damp smell of earth seemed to enhance the deepening chill. A slow fog soon settled in the lower grounds and swirled around the various headstones.

"Shadowy place," Watson, induced into a whisper by the surroundings, remarked.

"Yes, Watson, but I should think rather peaceful on a clear afternoon." I stopped abruptly, fancying I heard some noise not far off, but the lamps did not have great depth of penetration. Reflections off the mist made visibility null at any
great distance.

We pressed on and soon found ourselves at the gravesite. The grave remained open, a dark hole in the floor marked for a young Captain who had yet to accept this final invitation. The coffin rested nearby. "How is it," I asked our attendant, "that the grave remains open?"

"Rains, sir. Ground's too 'eavy to lift that muck back in. And, if I may say so, we've already dug that plot twice and judging from the looks of the two of you, gov', youda had me diggin' it up again tonight. As to the casket, nobody'd claimed it and seems a shame to bury it unoccupied. "

I had to admit that he had a point. We examined the grave but found nothing of interest in the empty hole.

"The casket," Watson suggested, "might that not be a source for those finger marks you've been working on?"

"*Fingerprints*, Watson. Sadly, no. No telling how many hands have touched the thing and, no doubt, this weather would have rendered any marks unrecoverable by now." We turned our attention to the interior of the box. The two men helped me pry open the lid. The lining was a bit soiled from the unusual amount of activity for the object. I probed the quilted lining with my cane and struck an object. "Hello. What do we have here? Bring the beam closer, Watson."

Using the stick I lifted the metallic object from the coffin. We had no time to examine it as we were abruptly interrupted by the sharp snap of a branch. We were not alone. I reacted instinctively by grabbing my friend's lamp, tossing it into the open grave while yelling, "Down, Watson!"

The caretaker was, unfortunately, frozen in his surprise. He made an easy target standing with his lantern stretched before him. We saw the muzzle flash just before we heard the crack of the rifle. The missile struck the caretaker in the chest, killing him instantly, we would soon learn, and knocked him back, and I am sad to say, ironically, into the gaping coffin. Watson fired a shot in the general direction of the attacker to let him know we had not come unarmed. With our lights extinguished there was no hope of pursuing the assassin through the darkened cemetery. I lit a match, allowing the Doctor a brief examination of the victim, but it was immediately clear that there was nothing that could be done for him. We closed the lid and picked our way carefully back toward the main gate.

The police were summoned to Brookwood and, when his men had finished their business, Lestrade escorted us back to Baker Street, our driver having fled at the first sign of commotion. Mrs Hudson had thoughtfully laid on a cold supper. I laid out the details of our investigation.

"Well, Mr Holmes, it shows how we investigators think alike. All along I suspected foul doings that went beyond a mere grave robbery." Lestrade sipped his ale as Watson and I exchanged knowing glances, all too familiar with the inspector's willingness to incorporate our work to his benefit. "Still, that does not answer the question of who is behind this?" Lestrade stating the obvious.

Mrs Hudson cleared the meal as we retired to review our information. "I almost forgot, Mr Holmes," she said, pulling an envelope from her apron. "This telegram came for you earlier."

"Thank you, dear lady. Try to get some rest now."

"I gave up on that long ago, knowing what these rooms are like once you and the Doctor get going on one of your romps. Victoria Station would be quieter." She took her leave.

I read the telegram to my guests, which confirmed my suspicions that Emmet-Jones's bank account had been emptied the day before his death. "Seems an unlikely coincidence that he would withdraw all of his funds the day before his death."

"How about blackmail?" Lestrade offered an unusually insightful suggestion.

"Yes, that is possible, Lestrade, yet who would have known he had any money? Clearly his means of support was derived through his marriage. No, there is something more. I cannot quite grasp the significance of the strange object we found in the coffin."

"Looks like some implement for cooking eggs," Lestrade commented.

"More like an odd fencing mask, I should think." I had to admit that I had reached a standstill in my deductions. The device, for it clearly had some purpose in its manufacture, was an oblong metallic structure seemingly like the frame of a handheld mirror without the glass. Attached to it by means of a hinge was a wire basket. It was then that Watson proved his worth as my able companion. "What do you make of it, Watson?" I called across the room as I held the object aloft.

Watson had left us and had been working at my chemistry bench for some time, so quietly that we had almost forgotten he was there. He had a text open in one hand and was mixing something over a flame. Nearby was the envelope that held the carpet samples extracted at Dunmore. Soon a noxious smoke began to emit from his experiment. This quickly began filling the room, forcing us to thrust open the windows to expel the foul cloud.

The stench and commotion drew another visit from our irate landlady. "What on earth are you men doing now?" she cried. "I shall never be able to get this odour out of these rooms."

We held kerchiefs over our mouths. It was some time before we were able to converse. "I think I used a bit too much alcoholic potash," Watson eventually explained, coughing and referring back to his text.

"I have to concur with Mrs Hudson. What *were* you doing there, good fellow?" I asked.

"You remember, Holmes, that the odour we encountered on the carpet at Dunmore, as well as in the coffin, seemed familiar. Well, it came to me during supper that the odour was chloroform. A vapour used as a modern anesthetic. The experiment there confirmed my suspicion. That device that we removed from the coffin is called Schimmelbusch's mask. It is a mechanism used to hold a chloroformed cloth in place over the patient's face while undergoing surgery. There are many devices used nowadays for such a purpose but this instrument is still in employ."

I could hardly contain my grin. I rushed across the room to shake the hand of my colleague. "Brilliant, Watson! We have our explanation."

Lestrade stood by with a look of confusion. "Explains what? I should like to know."

"It now becomes obvious, inspector. Both means and motive." I paused to light a pipe, both for dramatic effect and also in the hopes that the fragrant tobacco would serve to alleviate the rotten aroma unleashed by my friend's chemical foray. "What Watson has made plain is that Captain Emmet-Jones is not dead."

"The Devil, you say," Lestrade ejaculated.

"It would seem, my dear Lestrade, that Captain Emmet-Jones made the acquaintance of a young Doctor while in the service. He was engaged to a woman he did not love, but agreed to marry her to gain access to her wealth. He was in love with another, however."

"The maid, Nelly," Watson added.

"She was no more a maid than you or I, Watson. She was his lover." I withdrew the photograph that I had extracted from the desk at Dunmore. I had been careful not to let Lord Hemming observe it until we could be sure of the woman's role. "I am sure that this is she. As you can see by her dress, she was likely not wealthy, but certainly not of the servant class." Watson and Lestrade drew close to view the picture. "Once Emmet-Jones had Lord Hemming's money safely transferred to his personal account, he arranged to stage his own apparent demise by allowing his friend, our Dr Knox, to administer an anesthetic."

Watson continued the narrative. "To the casual observer, a deeply anesthetized subject may appear quite dead. Of course any physician worth his salt, such as Dr Sheridan, could easily tell, through auscultation with the stethoscope, that the heart was still beating, but Knox was already on hand and cleverly came up with the story of some contagious disease. This would ensure that the household, and no doubt a well-paid undertaker, kept a distance and excluded the possibility of holding a wake."

"From there," I resumed, "it would have been an easy matter to remove the body and rouse Emmet-Jones. When the exhumation was ordered it was assumed the body had been snatched from the grave, when, in reality, it was never present at the interment. The fact that the grave appeared undisturbed should have told you, Lestrade, that this was no routine act of robbery."

Lestrade looked down, ears turning a shade of red, but he said nothing at first. He then seemed to brighten and offered, "All we have to do is find this Dr Knox. We'll charge him with the murder of the caretaker. He'll sing a pretty tune and, I wager, turn Queen's evidence on the other two if faced with the gallows."

"The rifle that killed the caretaker no doubt will be of military issue," I added.

"You will find Knox all right," Watson said. "In a grave not far from the one slated for Emmet-Jones. He will have been dead nearly thirty years."

It was my turn to be astounded. "What are you saying, Watson?"

"While I pondered the connection between this Dr Knox and the grave robbery, something occurred to me. Do you remember the case of Messer's Hare and Burke, Holmes?"

I had to ponder for some moments, but then it struck me. "Yes, Watson, I believe you are correct." I explained for the perplexed inspector's benefit, "Hare and Burke were arrested for grave robbery some fifty years ago."

"There was a time, I shudder to say," Watson mused, "when cadavers for the education of medical students were in short supply. Often students had to resort to grave robbery to find specimens fresh enough for anatomic study. Must have been distasteful business. Soon a lucrative industry was born in the early part of the century in grave robbery to supply the medical profession. These men called themselves Ressurectionists, which, in some way, I suppose they were. Hare and Burke decided to run their own supply business out of their boarding home, later to be called by the locals, the Dead House. I must correct you here, Holmes. They were not grave robbers but murderers who sold the freshly killed bodies before they were buried."

"An even fresher supply, one would think," I said.

"Quite. Their arrest led to the Anatomy Act of 1832 which prohibited such activities as the plundering of graves for medical purposes."

"And the Doctor they supplied, Watson?" I asked, now knowing the likely response.

"Would be one Robert Knox. Brilliant anatomist who performed over five hundred anatomical dissections. Drew crowds from all over to watch his demonstrations, both medical and lay persons alike. He withdrew in some disgrace when the enterprise was revealed but while Burke hanged, Knox and Hare went free. Emmet-Jones's physician-friend had a sense of humour. He was mocking us all with his reference to Knox and must have thought he would never be found out."

"Easy to find him out," I said, "but I trust not easy to find."

I instructed Lestrade to contact army headquarters where the muster list of Emmet-Jones's regiment would no doubt reveal the true identity of our mystery Doctor. By then, if my Beekman's timetable was correct, the trio, for no doubt the woman in the photo they called 'Nelly' was with them, would be well out of the country via the Night Scotsman. I left Lestrade the task of tracking them further on the continent, letting him take the official credit if they could be found, and promised to break the news to Lord Hemming and his daughter.

While the official credit would go to no one, as the trio was never located, I was quick to applaud the work of my associate and am proud to publicly state it in these pages.

His reply, "Elementary, my dear Holmes," was well earned.

—Baker Street
London, 1904

✗

A LETTER FROM LEGRAND

A SEQUEL TO 'THE GOLD BUG'
BY EDGAR A. POE

by David Ellis

I had received no news from William Legrand since 1843. In the summer of that year relations between us had been abruptly severed when my erstwhile companion had taken grave offence at a fanciful account of our discovery of Captain Kidd's treasure in South Carolina that had appeared in a Philadelphia newspaper. He blamed me and in truth I could not disclaim all responsibility. For the several years since then no word had passed between us. I reflected often upon our momentous adventure if for no other reason than that my subsequent life has been mainly directed to the oversight of the investments that my portion of our find had allowed me to acquire, notably my latest handsome property here in Maryland, but about his later activities I had no knowledge.

Accordingly, my astonishment was considerable when, just three days ago, on my return from an unavoidable excursion to Washington, my major-domo informed me that awaiting my arrival was a young lady claiming to be the niece of William Legrand. She had given her name as Madeline de Freville.

Intriguing as this intelligence was, there was much other urgent business to claim my attention and I needed to also to bathe away the weariness of travel. I sent word that I was unable to receive her immediately but that I should be honoured if she would accept the hospitality of my house and join me at dinner.

That evening as I descended the broad staircase to the ground floor my ear was charmed by the gentle sounds of a piano. When I entered the music room a young woman arose from the keyboard in a rustle of silk and taffeta that shimmered in the warm candlelight. Small and slender, she was about four-and twenty, with a heart-shaped dark-eyed face framed by shining black hair.

"Miss de Freville?" said I as I took her hand. " I am sorry to have kept you waiting but I am now most happy to welcome you to my home."

The fervour of her response took me aback. "You cannot know how overjoyed I am to meet you at last!" she exclaimed. "There is so little time left!"

"But first I must give you these," she continued, taking some papers from a wooden box that lay on the piano top. They were letters of introduction from worthy citizens of New Orleans confirming that the bearer was indeed the daughter of a sister to William Legrand of that city.

"These all seem in order," I nodded as I returned the documents to her.

Miss de Freville extracted a small bright object from her reticule and offered it to me.

"You may find this a stronger testament to my identity," she said.

It was a man's gold signet ring, its circular face engraved with an intricate serpentine pattern. The last time I had seen this curious piece it had adorned the hand of Legrand. From my fob I lifted a gold seal and held it against the ring. The two gleaming faces matched exactly.

"These roundels were among Kidd's hoard," I explained. "Your uncle and I judged them to be from a pair of Spanish ear-rings. We took a fancy to them and retained one each as particular mementos of our discovery."

She nodded. "So he told me when he gave the ring to me."

Her credentials thus established I offered Miss de Freville a glass of amontillado, led her to an elegant French chair and sought more information.

"And what of your uncle?" I inquired when she was settled. "You may know that there have been no exchanges between us for many years."

A shadow seemed to fall across her face. "He gave me that ring in the foreknowledge of his impending death," she said sombrely. "I am sorry to tell you that a few weeks ago he was consigned to the family tomb."

"But Legrand was not an old man," I exclaimed. "Was he ill, then?"

"In a way," she replied softly. "I profoundly regret that I bring you sad news but you must know everything. My uncle took his own life with a duelling pistol. Moreover, as if that were not calamity enough, he dealt a further terrible blow to the family. Possessed by some crochet, before he died he hid all his wealth deriving form his share of the treasure you found together. Now it is no one knows where." A desperate tremor entered her voice. "Unless you can help me it will be lost forever and my family condemned to undeserved penury!"

Madeline de Freville told me her remarkable story as we dined. Even during the brief period I had been close to him Legrand was always subject to violent swings of mood, at times lively and enthusiastic but at others deep in dejection. Later, it seemed, he had become increasingly misanthropic, regarding his fellow man with a mixture of suspicion and contempt. Every slight, real or imagined, fed his mistrust and prejudice. What he saw as my betrayal he had taken as one more evidence of the perfidy of those around him. More and more that black melancholy I remembered so well came to dominate his days and nights. As had happened before, he had withdrawn from the world and become estranged from his family, with the sole exception of Madeline.

"I am the only child of his youngest sister," she explained. "My mother died in the year after you recovered the treasure. My uncle took me under his wing and appeared to reserve for me a little at least of the affection he denied to others. In recent years the rest of the family have fallen on evil times. A ship bearing our cargo was lost, a local bank foundered, a crop we were counting on failed. But my uncle remained unmoved. Throughout all he stayed aloof and withheld his help."

"I am greatly saddened by what you tell me," I said. "Evidently wealth did not bring your uncle the fulfilment that has come to me. I have long regretted that my imprudence brought about our bitter separation. Otherwise—who can say?—I might have been able to prevent his sorry decline."

I recounted to Miss de Freville what had occurred to drive a wedge between me and her uncle. In 1842 I had been residing near Philadelphia. At a dinner party one evening I had been persuaded to give an account to the company of the unearthing of Kidd's booty through Legrand's brilliant analysis of the old pirate's cipher, found by chance on the Carolina shore. The wine had flowed freely on that occasion and I gave perhaps the fullest exposition of my adventure that I had ever provided. I had assumed, of course, that my auditors were all men of honour. I paid no special regard to a stranger in our number, the guest of one of my friends, save to remark in his physiognomy an uncommon breadth of brow and in his manner an unwarranted disdain. Only later did I recall how intent had been his pale face in the glow from the candles as he listened to my narrative.

"You may imagine," I declared to Miss de Freville "both my astonishment and outrage a year afterwards when my attention was drawn to a sensational tale entitled 'The Gold Bug' in a local public newspaper setting out a lurid version of the account I had given. The author had not even attempted to conceal his identity and his dishonour. He was Edgar Allan Poe, that guest at my table, and as the world now knows from the Reverend Griswold, a notorious wastrel and shameless villain.

"I wrote to your uncle to inform him of what had happened and entreating his forgiveness. He rejected my explanation. In vain did I point out that I, too, had cause to be angry. Not only for Poe's breach of trust, but because by presenting his tale as the narrative of your uncle's companion Poe made his wretched fictional elaborations appear to come from me. Your uncle replied coldly that he could no longer consider me his friend and that henceforward there would be no further communication between us. It was the saddest moment of my life. From that time I have cursed the name of Edgar Poe!"

"My uncle did not forget you," said Miss de Freville. "You were much in his thoughts before he died. Indeed, that is why I am here."

Her words reminded me of the questions I had not yet put to her. For what purpose had she sought me? What had she meant by her passionate cry that time was running out?

She agreed to my suggestion that we adjourn to the library, breaking away only for a moment to reclaim from the music room the box I had remarked earlier. My ample book-lined chamber is where I retire when I need to retreat from the humdrum affairs of the day and require a haven of calm in which to reflect. As well as a collection of volumes as rich as any in the state, it has many reminders of earlier times. One of the walls bears a portrait of William Legrand together with some of his own fine sketches of shells and lepidoptera. Displayed, too, is a navigators' chart of Sullivan's Island where Legrand, living like a recluse, had had his refuge and from where, in accordance with Captain Kidd's enigmatic directions, we had embarked on our expedition to the mainland. Miss de Freville stood for a long moment before the brooding stillness of her uncle's striking picture.

"That was painted shortly after our exploit," I said. "It is an excellent likeness."

"I am glad to have seen it" said she " for my most recent memories of him recall a sadder man whose soul was darkened by bitterness."

She sank gracefully into the chair I indicated and I invited her to continue her story.

"If my uncle's death—and the dreadful manner of it—came as shocks to the family, the revelations that followed left us all thunderstricken. For his attorney told us that my uncle's fortune had disappeared. Or should I say rather it had been spirited away!"

I was astonished. "How could that be?"

"In the weeks before his death my uncle had roused himself from his melancholic lethargy and become very busy. Characteristically he told no-one what he was about and the family assumed he was devoting himself once more to the matters he had long neglected. How little we knew! In fact, as the lawyer now informed us he had been converting his property into cash but what he had done with the funds was not known. They seemed to have entirely vanished." She paused. "When the will was read the only bequest was made to me. It comprised this little box and certain documents within it."

This was my chance to examine the receptacle Miss de Freville had brought with her. It was about a foot long, four inches tall and five inches across. The wood was unfamiliar to me, being dark, shiny and with a spicy aroma akin to sandalwood. The lid was curved but with a flattened top. This uppermost surface was criss-crossed with silver wire and in the lozenge-shaped panels thus formed was the name LEGRAND in brass characters standing slightly proud. At the front a key of curious design protruded from an elaborate escutcheon. The whole appearance of this object was very singular and somehow rather sinister.

"What is its history?" I asked.

Madeline de Freville shook her head. "It has been in my uncle's possession for many years. He kept it in his study. It is believed he had it made on one of his journeys long ago though no one now recalls when or where it came from."

"And the documents in the box?" I prompted.

"There was first a codicil to the will declaring that my uncle's wealth had been deposited at locations he forebore to disclose. It would come to me, but only if I could discover the hiding places within six months and a day. If the money was not found then it would rot where it lay. The box also held a sealed letter with your name on it. I was instructed to deliver it to you and enlist your help in the search."

"And how did you find me?"

"It took time," she said. "I knew, of course, that you had once lived in Charleston and my uncle's papers included a record of your later address in Philadelphia. I had enquiries made in both places. While this was taking place I was very conscious of the passing weeks and of the pressing needs of my family. My relief at eventually finding your new home here was replaced by despair on learning that you were away on business." Her eyes widened in urgent appeal. "Oh, it is not for myself that I am concerned. There are my aunts, my cousins and others who will suffer. This perverse punishment is so unfair. He would not acknowledge it but they truly shared my affection for my uncle. With the bequest I can help them. I can try to rebuild the run-down estate and re-establish my family's position. Much is at stake and of the time allowed me only a few weeks remain."

Now I understood her emotion at my return home. "Your tale is certainly extraordinary," I declared, greatly moved by her words. "And I am most eager to see the letter you have striven so hard to deliver to me."

She lifted from the box a folded paper. It bore only my name, written in a bold black script I had not seen for so many years. I broke the seal and read William Legrand's letter. I did not know what to expect. Indeed, I had not thought ever to have received any message from him again. When I had finished, my opinion was that his letter was second only to Captain Kidd's cryptic parchment as the most memorable document I had ever clapped eyes upon:

> To my old companion, a most warm salutation.
>
> So my kinswoman has found you. My congratulations on an auspicious start, though I did not doubt that such sharp wits would triumph. I am profoundly sorry that an old rift has put us apart for so long. But, by your own admission, it was your folly that brought it about. Now I grant you an opportunity to annul that old wrong. To borrow words from a scribbling blackguard, I punish you in my own way by a bit of mystification.
>
> Long ago—with your aid—I found Kidd's booty, but now my spirit has a loathing for that sinful hoard. At first I had thought simply to consign it back to oblivion. But as my kinfolk clamour for it I confront my family and you with your own hunt for gold. For it is now hid away again and your task is to bring it to light.
>
> With what is in your hands you can find what was my portion of Kidd's loot. Call to mind again our days on Sullivan's Island and what I taught you in my old hut. Finally, I grant you this nominal hint: what is sought you will find through what is not found.
>
> Good hunting.

There followed Legrand's sprawling signature.

Wordlessly I passed the paper to Madeline de Freville who scanned it closely. When she looked up her face was clouded with disappointment.

"But this does not help us! There is no indication of where my uncle's wealth might be."

"Seemingly not," I agreed. "At least not directly. Tell me, do you recognise the writing as that of your uncle?"

"Oh yes," she nodded. "Why do you ask?"

"Well," said I. "In the tone of this letter I seem to hear once more your uncle's sardonic humour. Yet the style seems awkward in a way I cannot precisely fathom. Perhaps it reflects his state of mind at the time of writing."

Miss de Freville turned to me imploringly.

"What are we to do?" she cried. "If the bequest is not claimed within the next few weeks it will be beyond reach. To have endured so much—the death of my uncle, his extraordinary will, my search for you—and still to be no nearer saving my family!"

She had every reason to be distraught, and the strain I had earlier perceived was close to overwhelming her.

"My dear Madeline," I said. "All is not lost. This letter purports to offer pointers to where your fortune is to be found, clews which I am charged to solve. I recollect that once before I received from your uncle a note that gave me great uneasiness. It proved to be the direct precursor to the adventure that changed my life. Therefore, let me consider this document further. We shall speak again in the morning. In the meantime I earnestly entreat you to get some rest."

At length Miss de Freville consented to retire and, alone in the library, I reviewed the story she had told me. Fantastic certainly, but not out of character for William Legrand as I had known him. While it was shocking that he should torment those closest to him, more puzzling perhaps was why he should involve me in what appeared to be a family matter. Had it been in his mind simply to cause me discomfiture by reviving our old quarrel? Or had he felt some impulse to re-establish contact between us but, constrained by his perverse and wayward nature, been compelled to resort to this bizarre indirect course? In any event, I concluded, everything I now possessed flowed from Legrand's recruitment of me in his astonishing expedition into the Carolina wilderness years ago. I had no choice now but to do whatever I could to comply with his wishes.

I poured a glass of brandy and looked again at the letter. "With what is in your hand you can find what was my portion of Kidd's loot." That at least was clear enough. The letter was itself the key. It must contain some covert message. However, while Legrand had delighted in such contrivances he had been well aware of my own lack of expertise in such matters.

Wait, now! I was not entirely ignorant. I knew a little. I knew what Legrand had told me himself! Once more I surveyed the cryptic document. "I bid you call to mind again our days on Sullivan's Island and what I taught you in my old hut." I raised my eyes to Legrand's portrait. "But you told so much, my friend," I murmured. "And it was long ago."

There was no record of what had been said in Legrand's se-
cluded cabin on his sandy refuge, only my fading memories. The
painted gaze of the picture's deep-set eyes seemed to bore into my
skull. Wait again! There was a record of a sort. And Legrand himself referred to it. "Words from a scribbling blackguard." Could
it be that he was deliberately calling to my attention that tale by
Edgar Poe, the cause of our separation?

And I had a copy. When at first the journal had come into my
possession I had crumpled it in bitter fury. I had not looked at it
since heaven knew when but I knew where it lay. It was the work
of moments to reclaim it from the bottom drawer of the secretaire.
I spread the brittle pages with care upon the leather surface of my
desk.

The paper was yellowing but the print was perfectly legible. The
Dollar Newspaper No 23 Vol 1, Philadelphia, Wednesday Morn-
ing, June 28 1843. A Family Periodical—Devoted to Literature,
Domestic and Foreign News, Agriculture, Education, Finance,
Amusements &c—Independent On All Subjects.

The front page, seven columns wide, was almost entirely taken
up by Poe's text. It was claimed as an original story which—and
this I remembered had been particularly galling to me—had been
awarded a prize. Doubts assailed me. Could this wretched stuff
really unlock the mystery? But what alternative did I have? I read
the story from beginning to end.

My emotions were mixed. The faults in the story were many—
the nonsense about the non-existent golden insect; the transforma-
tion of Legrand's devoted manservant into a buffoon; the vastly
exaggerated scale and value of what we found. Nevertheless, Poe
had captured the extraordinary atmosphere surrounding those far-
off events—the bleakness of Sullivan's Island with the constant
surf and pervading scent of myrtle, and the wildness of the craggy
wooded Carolina tableland. He had caught, too, Legrand's nervous
excitement and my own bafflement during our journey, our weary-
ing dig by lantern-light, and the thrill and wonder of the eventual
discovery. More relevant to my present purpose, with great clarity
Poe had set out the steps of Legrand's decipherment of Kidd's message, and I hoped my reviving memories would help to stimulate
my wits to benefit from these details.

I paused twice in my reading. First at these words: "… it may well be doubted whether human ingenuity can construct an enigma of the kind which human ingenuity may not, by proper application, resolve." The sentence may have been Poe's own—at this remove I could not remember—but the sentiment had certainly been shared by my friend. Could I now live up to this daunting challenge? Secondly, close to the end of Poe's story, I found the source of Legrand's quotation from it: " I felt somewhat annoyed by your evident suspicions touching my sanity, and so resolved to punish you quietly, in my own way, by a little bit of sober mystification." That Legrand should borrow this phrase from Poe's story endorsed my intuition that it must hold the key to the puzzle he had set for me.

For a second time I read the story, concentrating my attention on the latter part of the narrative, Legrand's unravelling of Kidd's conundrum, for this was the closest I could get to "what I taught you in my old hut." From his first recognition of the death's-head drawing through to the interpretation of the idiosyncratic directions to the precise location of the pirate's buried chest, each step of Legrand's reasoning was there.

A little way into Poe's version I was struck by these words: "You are well aware that chemical preparations exist, and have existed time out of mind, by means of which it is possible to write upon either paper or vellum, so that the characters shall become visible only when subjected to the action of fire. Zaffre, digested in *aqua regia,* and diluted with four times its weight of water, is sometimes employed; a green tint results. The regulus of cobalt, dissolved in spirits of nitre, gives a red. These colours disappear at longer or shorter intervals after the material written upon cools, but again become apparent upon the re-application of heat."

This was surely the answer! It was, after all, by this means that Legrand had first revealed the writing on Kidd's parchment. He must have used his arcane knowledge to insert some invisible message between the lines of his script to me. True, I could discern no trace of additional penwork but I was convinced I had penetrated Legrand's "mystification."

I pressed his letter to the warm lamp, eagerly awaiting the emergence of the secret text, but nothing happened. I tried again with a candle, playing the flame gently over each surface of the document. But no writing appeared, whether tinted green or red or anything else. I was on a false trail.

For a third time I perused the story. On this reading, some halfway into the account of Legrand's explanation, a statement brought me up short. I turned once more to my old friend's letter and re-examined it with great care. I thrilled to find my suspicion confirmed. Here was something most extraordinary, even, according to Legrand's own dictum, virtually impossible. From one mystery I was being led to another.

Next morning I descended early to the breakfast room where I partook gratefully of hot fresh coffee. Madeline de Freville soon joined me.

"I barely slept," she declared. "Please tell me, do you have any news?"

"Since you must be fatigued," I replied " you should first break your fast." I indicated a covered plate set at her place.

"Oh, I cannot eat," said she. "I am too anxious."

"I insist," I said. "Indeed, my dear, I shall tell you nothing until you have sampled what has been put out for you."

Seeing that I was resolute on this point she sat down. Her face was a study as she raised the silver cover to reveal a long envelope upon the plate. The blood drained from her cheeks. "What is this?" she whispered.

"Since it is addressed to you," I answered. "I have not opened it. But my surmise is that it contains the whereabouts of your uncle's bequest to you."

I was unprepared for her reaction to my statement. Her eyelids fluttered and to my great alarm she fell back in her chair in a swoon. Cursing myself I sprang to her side. I chafed her wrists and to my considerable relief her eyes soon opened.

"That was unpardonable of me, Madeline," I said contritely. "I cannot apologise enough for such a prank."

She smiled weakly. "I assure you I am quite recovered. It is just that I have had so many shocks in so brief a time."

While I poured her coffee she reached for the envelope and slit it open with trembling fingers. She studied the documents she found within then held them out to me. In brief, they were addressed by William Legrand to lawyers in Richmond and Washington instructing them to hand over to Madeline de Freville or her accredited representative the sealed boxes he had deposited with them on specified occasions. Madeline would be able to restore her family's fortunes.

"I do not understand," she cried. "Where have these papers come from?"

I produced her uncle's box and the letter she had given me the previous evening.

"From these," I said.

She shook her head in wonderment. "You must explain."

Seeing that she was almost overcome with impatience for a solution to this most perplexing riddle, I, emulating Legrand himself years earlier, entered into a full detail of the circumstances connected with it.

"Very well. Your uncle set us each a task. Yours was to find me. Mine was to uncover the route to his legacy. Your uncle wrote that it could be found "with what is in your hands." All we held were the letter itself and the box that had contained it. Accordingly, my conviction grew that these two items somehow held the answer."

She nodded eagerly. "Go on."

"I followed Legrand's guidance. His advice in his letter to me, you recall, is to remember what he taught me on Sullivan's Island. He also subtly reminded me that if my memory was defective I could find assistance in Edgar Poe's account of our adventure." I showed Madeline the significant words in her uncle's letter and produced my copy of *The Dollar Newspaper*.

"One thing Legrand had explained to me after we found the treasure was that the key to Kidd's cipher lay in the frequency with which the letters of the alphabet normally appear in an English text. Here is how Mr Poe expressed it:

"Now, in English, the letter which most frequently occurs is E. Afterwards the succession runs thus: a o i d h n r s t u y c f g l m w b k q x z. E predominates so remarkably that an individual sentence of any length is rarely seen in which it is not the prevailing character.

"Look again at that singular message of your uncle's. Except in the signature it does not contain the letter E at all! That is the reason for the stilted style. He was constrained by the limitations of not employing any word with E in it. For example, he does not refer to you by name or describe you as his niece. It is also why when he quoted from Poe's story he did not do so exactly—he was obliged to omit the words that include E."

Madeline scrutinised the letter anew and satisfied herself of the veracity of my statements.

"I am vexed that I did not observe this for myself," said she. "But I remain at a loss to imagine what it could mean."

I resumed my explanation. "Your uncle went on to say that I should seek what is not found. Since what we cannot find in his note is the letter E then that is what I had to look for. At length I realised that staring me in the face was the capital E among the brass letters here on the lid of his box. These are the letters of his name and thus my hypothesis is confirmed when I recall Legrand described his hint as "nominal," meaning on this occasion literally pertaining to a name—his name.

"Once my attention had been directed to the box the obvious inference to be drawn was that it had a concealed compartment access to which is controlled by the brass E. You see how the letters stand proud. My first thought was pressing down on the E was required. But this yielded no result and on reflection it was hardly a reasonable theory since any chance knock might inadvertently operate the mechanism. Nor could I shift it in any sidewise direction. The only possibility remaining was that the letter must be pulled up further from the surface. Now, apply these small pincers and attempt to draw the E outwards."

As she did so there was a click as the metal rose about an eighth of an inch and a muffled clatter sounded within. She raised the lid to reveal that its inner surface had swung down to disclose a shallow padded recess. Marvelling at the intricate mechanism she played with the box like a fascinated child, closing and releasing the artfully fashioned hiding place.

"How ingenious of Uncle William to devise such a puzzle." She looked up. "And how clever of you to solve it."

I demurred. "No, my dear. I should have seen the answer far quicker than I did. Your uncle's "nominal" hint pointed clearly to it. And consider: your family come from Huguenot stock. In French "le grand" may mean "the great" as, for example, "Alexandre le

Grand" denotes "Alexander the Great." But if I set it out like this, what could you have?"

She studied what I had written. "'L'E grand.' Why, that might possibly be taken to mean capital E!"

I nodded. "E is not only within your uncle's name, it is the one letter that could be signified by it. In every way, you see, the key to your fortune lay in a letter from Legrand."

Madeline de Freville has left now, gone on the concluding stages of her quest. Though her stay was brief the house sees strangely empty without her. I hope she will return one day as she promised to do when she took her leave.

Again she had thanked most warmly for unravelling her uncle's conundrum.

"I wish it were possible to thank Edgar Poe also," she added. "For was it not his story that led you to the solution."

"Indeed it was," I acknowledged. "They say he had a strong sense of irony. It is certainly ironic that the man who caused the rift between your uncle and me should have brought us together, albeit in so strange a manner. Perhaps somewhere his shade has observed our little mystery with approval."

Madeline will soon have her inheritance. But I have not gone unrewarded. For I had not told her that there had been another enclosure in that ingenious box. It lies before me now, a small slip on which are set down above her uncle's distinctive signature, seven short lines of curious symbols. These I recognised at once as the characters devised by Captain Kidd for his cipher. For convenience I transcribe them below using the signs employed by Edgar Poe for our nineteenth-century printing press as follows:

```
9:†85(1(68*†
61:‡?(8:8))?(¶8:;48)806*8);48*:‡?
45¶8)‡0¶8†9:9:);616-5;6‡*
9:485(;68);-‡*3(5;?05;6‡*)
6†8-05(8;45;‡?(†6118(8*-8)5(8
(8)‡0¶8†5*†5006)1‡(36¶8*
1‡;4805);;6983‡‡†2:8
```

Although this new enigma had been unexpected I was confident that I could unravel it. And, indeed, following Legrand's methodology, it was the work of minutes for me to reveal his final message:

> My dear friend
>> If your eyes survey these lines then you have solved my mystification. My heartiest congratulations. I declare that our differences are resolved and all is forgiven. For the last time,
>> Goodbye
>>> William Legrand

With strong emotions I had raised a glass to the portrait in my library. As much as Madeline prizes the riches that await her, far more do I hold dear this final letter from Legrand.

✗

The management evaluations were toughening.

AN OLD-FASHIONED VILLAIN

by Nick Andreychuk

Desiree fought back the wave of nausea that washed over her body. The dry cloth that was stuffed between her teeth would undoubtedly block any vomit from exiting, causing her to slowly choke to death on her own bile. It was possible she'd die soon anyway, but she had no intentions of letting *fear* be the instrument of her demise.

Desiree felt tied in such a way that she could barely move. The blindfold that pushed cruelly against her eyeballs made it difficult to determine where she was. She could tell from the warm breeze and fresh scent of manure that she was outdoors, and she knew that it was Michael who had brought her here . . . but she knew nothing else. She could only imagine what she was lying on—two hard, slender rods digging painfully into her shoulders and knees. Her head lay on what felt like hundreds of sharp stones.

Suddenly, the ground shook beneath her.

The intensity of the vibrations increased steadily, and it felt as if something immense was heading her way.

It was all Desiree could do not to give in to the hysteria that threatened to take over her mind. Being eighteen, she knew she was unlikely to have a heart attack, yet she didn't see how her heart could continue to function at the frenetic pace it was beating.

In the distance, she heard a loud whistle—a sound that was all too familiar from the years spent living near a railroad station. A sound that, when combined with the rail-like objects beneath her, left little doubt as to where she was . . . and how short her life expectancy was.

"Mmmph!" Desiree tried to call out to her captor, but the gag muffled her attempts. *Michael!* she screamed in her mind. *What the hell is wrong with you?*

Was she bait to lure her boyfriend Dylan to some violent, macho showdown? But what if Dylan didn't show? Would Michael leave her here to die?

She could hear the *clickity-clack clickity-clack* of the train getting closer.

Desiree realized with sudden certainty that Dylan wasn't coming. Michael was possessive and quick-tempered, but he wasn't stupid—he had to know that Desiree would never choose him just because he'd beaten Dylan in physical combat. So the only logical, *terrifying* reason for him to bring her here was to dispose of her. She had no doubt that he was deranged enough to enact the adage, "If I can't have her, *nobody* will. . . ."

The noise from the oncoming train became all encompassing. Any second now it would smash right into her . . .

Desiree's bladder let go just as the train blasted past her, mere inches from the top of her head.

After several minutes, Desiree started to relax. Maybe that bastard Michael had just wanted to scare her. Maybe —

The ground began to shake again, and though the sound of the second train was still far away, the rails beneath her were already shaking much more violently than the first time.

⚔

THE PREMATURE MURDER

by Michael Mallory

If ever I needed a drink to calm my nerves, it was now.

On this stiflingly hot August afternoon in the year of our lord 1852, I strode into The Town Crier, reputed to be the oldest tavern in the city of Baltimore, not knowing whether I was going to be afforded respect for holding onto my principals as a gentleman, or whether I would soon join the ranks of the city's unemployed. It had certainly not been my intention upon entering the private office of Mr. Samuel Bellwether to deliver a heated tirade upon my increasingly frustrating situation; I merely let my head get away from me. But I had a genuine grievance: I had been a part of the Bellwether Detective Agency for three months and I had yet to be assigned a case of any kind. The agency's other operatives were all out on the job, in some cases multiple jobs, while I remained a glorified office boy. I suspected I knew why: like Old Sam Bellwether himself the others were former police officers, recruited from various constabularies, whilst I was a West Point man with no official police experience. Yet how was I expected to gain experience if I spent all my time in the office organizing files?

I ordered a beer and stood at the bar, silently ruminating about my problem, when I heard a voice calling my name from the other end of the tavern. Looking up, I was rather startled to see the open, friendly face of a man who had been a cadet with me at the Point. "Tom Macgowan," I called back, "is that you?"

"It is!" he said, charging like a bull in my direction. "What on earth are you doing here?

I clasped his hand. "I might ask you the same."

"Don't you read the *American and Commercial Advisor*?"

"I do not. Do you work on the paper?"

"Work on it?" he cried. "I will have you know I am the paper's star reporter. Of course, my editors do not realize that yet, which is why I find myself writing death notices and accounts of church socials."

I laughed heartily. "We share a predicament! I happen to be the best operative in the Bellwether Detective Agency, though my superior believes that my true talents lie in keeping track of the files and fetching him growlers of ale whenever his throat dries."

"Here's to Baltimore's most underappreciated gentlemen," Tom said, raising his glass to me.

Tom and I spent the remainder of the afternoon drinking, talking, laughing, and reliving our cadet days. As the clock tolled six, Tom set his glass down and said: "Great God, I just realized that I am supposed to be at work this evening. After what I have consumed, I hope I can find the offices again."

Tom suggested that we make a pact to meet at the tavern at least once a week, and after I agreed, he lurched out into the sultry evening. I, meanwhile, made up my mind to return to Mr. Bellwether's office and beg his forgiveness for my impetuosity. As I stood there, however, I heard a strange, whispery voice beside me say: "Did I hear you correctly, sir, that you work for a detective agency?"

I turned and saw a small man with a lined, weathered face, rheumy eyes and a gin-blossom nose. I judged him to be roughly seventy years of age, though possibly younger but marked by hard living. The dark suit he wore was shabby, threadbare, and not in a clean state, though somehow he managed to inhabit it with autumn dignity.

"You heard correctly, sir. Is it of some concern to you?"

"Only in that I find myself in need of your help. It is my son, you see."

"Your son is in trouble?"

"He is dead."

"I am sorry."

"His death was my fault."

I studied the man's face more closely. "You mean that you killed him?"

"I did nothing intentionally to hurt him. But my presence in his life ended it as effectively as though I had plunged a dagger into his heart with this hand."

That would have been difficult, I saw, since the hand he presented to me was maimed, having but two fingers, and unnaturally red in color. The old man caught my stare. "I used to make a living with these hands, as a cardsharp," he said. "But now..." He thrust his damaged hand into his pocket and with the other, raised his glass to his lips. After draining it, he asked: "Have you ever heard of an actor named Danton Prince?"

"I do not frequent the theatre."

"Even if you were, I daresay you would not be familiar with me."

"You were speaking of your son, Mr. Prince?"

Gazing at me blearily, he said: "Have you experienced the crashing realization that you have made the most grievous error possible?"

I said nothing, and he continued.

"Many years ago I rose from my bed having listened for most of the night to the caterwauling of my third child, and the distraught sobbing of its mother. At that moment I realized I was not meant to be a husband and father, so I disappeared into the night and fled."

"You walked out on your family?"

"I know it sounds heartless and perhaps it was, but I was young and ambitious, and I felt like I was being entombed by responsibility. I contrived to falsify the report of my death and assumed a new identity under which to resume my career. After my wife died my children were all raised by adoptive families. Then three years ago I presented myself to my middle son."

"And you say that led to his death?"

Instead of speaking, Danton Price began to examine his empty glass, as artful an act of begging as I had ever seen. After I paid for a fresh drink for him he resumed his tale. "The last decade has been harsh," he said. "I began to accrue gambling debts on so many fronts that threats were being made against me. Some were carried out..." he held his maimed hand before me once more "... and some were not, as the fact that I stand here before you, still drawing breath, confirms. Threats were made on my life. I knew I was being followed, watched. My situation was becoming so precarious that I had but one option left, which was to seek out my son and beg him for assistance."

The old man downed the remainder of his drink and I resolved not to buy him another.

"He was not difficult to find," Prince went on. "In the intervening years, he had achieved some renown as a man of letters.

I caught up with him here in Baltimore, steeled my nerve, and introduced myself."

"How did he accept the news of your existence?"

"As would anyone who is confronted by a ghost," Prince replied. "But Eddie possessed an extreme sense of irony, so once he recovered from the shock he congratulated me on the joke I had perpetrated upon the world. He possessed an even greater sense of honor, and he offered to help me. He allowed me to stay with him in the room he was letting while in Baltimore, and even gave me his own clothes, which were in far more reputable shape than those I was wearing. I wear them to this day." He ran his hands lovingly over his shabby suit. "He confessed to having little love for the foster father who raised him, and viewed my resurrection, as it were, as a chance to finally be a good and proper son. And how did I repay his kindness? By propelling him into the grave."

I was beginning to think that I was being led down a path with this tale of woe. "Mr. Prince," I said, "I beg you to explain yourself more succinctly. How did you propel your son into the grave?"

"I told you that he gave me his clothing, have I not?" he said. "My son stripped down to his undergarments right then and there and handed them to me. But that left him with nothing to wear, since he had only recently arrived in Baltimore and had not yet removed his steamer trunk out of storage at the dock. So he donned the clothes I had been wearing, which made him look like a tramp, and set out for the dock to facilitate the delivery of his trunk. He never returned. After four agonizing days, I learned of his death."

"I still fail to see any trace of your involvement," I declared.

"Can you not understand?" the old man cried. "He was wearing my clothing! We were of similar build and visage. Those who were following me, wishing to do me harm, mistook my son for me. *My boy was murdered in my place*!" His impassioned voice immediately gave way to a fit of violent coughing, and it did not take a detective to see that the man was unwell. "I do not believe I have long left," he whispered upon regaining control. "I wish the matter to be resolved before I die. I beg you to help me."

"What is it you want me to do, Mr. Prince?"

"Avenge my son. Bring his killer, or killers, to justice. Incidentally Prince is not my real name. It is Poe, sir. David Poe."

"Poe, you say?"

"Yes. My son was Edgar Allan Poe."

"**H**ell, junior, you've been flim-flammed!" Jed Hadley cried after I had proposed to Samuel Bellwether that I officially take up the case David Poe had put before me. Hadley was another operative and while he was no more than ten years older than I, he strode around as though he carried in his hat all the knowledge in the world. "You said the man was an actor. What you saw was a command performance!"

"Initially I thought the same thing," I said, turning my attention to Old Sam Bellwether, who was rocking back and forth in a creaking chair behind his desk. "But I investigated what the old man told me. Edgar Allen Poe did indeed die here under mysterious circumstances in 1849."

"What of it?" Hadley argued. "That in no way proves the old tosspot who conned you out of a drink was his father."

"How else would you explain the accuracy of his details regarding his son's death?" I countered, struggling to hold my temper.

"How do you know those details were so blasted accurate?" growled Pete Curlowe, another operative. Somewhere on the far side of fifty, Curlowe was built like a rock outcrop and he had a stony, expressionless face; even on those rare occasions when he laughed, Curlowe's visage never changed.

"I discovered that an old friend of mine works for the *Advisor*," I stated. "I consulted him and provided me with information about Poe's death, based upon the newspaper accounts."

"Oh, I see," Hadley said, grinning snidely. "And it never occurred to you that the old man could have gotten the same information from the same newspaper and parroted it back to you."

"All right, fellows, that's enough," Mr. Bellwether said. "Jed, Pete, go on back to work. I'll talk to the lad." After Hadley and Curlowe had gone, Old Sam closed the door to his private office and then sat back down in his ancient, creaking chair. "I know those two are not always easy to take," he said, "but they do have a point."

"So you believe I was taken in as well, sir?" I felt more chastened than defiant.

"Maybe you were spoon-fed a nonesuch and maybe you weren't. But even if the old man was telling the truth, how would we collect payment for the job? You described him as destitute."

"If payment is the only obstacle, Mr. Bellwether, I would be happy to take on the case on my own time, outside of my duties here."

"Why would you do that?"

"Because if I am successful, it will prove to you that I am ready for a case of my own."

"I see." Old Sam leaned back in the ancient chair. "Look son, I hired you because I saw the seed of a good operative somewhere inside you. God knows you've got the gumption. But you've also got a temper, and that's not a prime asset for a detective. When you can convince me that you can control that head of yours, we'll talk about a case. Now then, go down to the Crier and fetch me a growler. Make sure you're back by four o'clock."

"Sir, if you would only—" I began, but then silenced myself, uncertain I had heard him correctly. Pulling out my repeater, I saw that it was just past one. "I'm sorry, Mr. Bellwether, did you say four o'clock?"

"I did. Until then you are on your own time. Unless that's a problem."

"No sir, not at all," I said, unable to suppress a grin. "Thank you, Mr. Bellwether." I dashed out of his office and walked past Hadley and Curlowe, I bid them both as cheerful a good afternoon as I could muster and then left the premises. Striding happily down Ashland Street for several blocks, I suddenly stopped. My elation at having been offered a chance to prove myself had completely clouded the fact that I had not the slightest whit of an idea how to proceed. After standing stupidly for a few moments, trying to collect my wits, I opted for heading to the place of my primary source of information, the offices of the *Advisor*, where I sought out Tom Macgowan.

"I sensed you would be back," he said, greeting me in the lobby of the building. "Come with me, I have something for you." He led me back to his desk, and from it picked up an envelope and handed it to me. "I was able to unearth more information concerning your Mr. Poe. I have culled together some clippings for you. It is not much, I'm afraid, but you are welcome to it."

"This is wonderful," I said, opening the envelope and fingering the small stack of newspaper cuttings and handwritten notes. "I owe you something for this, Tom."

"Indeed you do," he replied. "Dinner this Saturday would suffice."

After leaving Tom to his work, I hastened to the Town Crier in the hopes that old Mr. Poe might be there. Alas, he was not. Taking a corner table, I pored over the clippings, which revealed Edgar Allan Poe to be a troubled and troubling man with a weakness for drink and a singular lack of friends. Obsessed with mystery during his life, Poe had managed to deliver one at the threshold of death. According to the notes, the dying author had repeatedly called out the name *Reynolds*, the significance of which no one could state. Accepting his father's presumption that he was indeed murdered, it could have been the name of his killer, though it was hardly efficacious to track down everyone in the city named "Reynolds" and ask them if they were responsible. The only truly useful piece of information to be gleaned from the cuttings was that a physician named Dr. John J. Moran attended Poe in his final, delusional hours.

A glance at my repeater told me it was nearly half past three; my free time was nearly over. I moved to the bar and placed Old Sam's order for ale with the barkeep, who, as he drew the amber liquid into the glass jug, instructed me to remind my boss that payment was past due on his tab. I agreed, but in exchange extracted a return favor: should the man who called himself Danton Prince return to the tavern, he was to be instructed to come immediately to the Bellwether Detective Agency offices and ask for me.

The rest of the day passed unceremoniously, and a bit after seven, I left for home. I had gone no further than a half-mile from the Agency when I heard rushing footsteps and then experienced something being violently pulled down over my head! It was a foul-smelling canvas sack that constricted my breathing. Even so, I did not panic. I attempted to lash out with my fist, hoping to strike my assailant, but as I did so powerful arms wrapped themselves around mine and held them behind my back. A second set of arms grabbed me around the waist and dragged me off of the sidewalk. I attempted to shout, but little sound emerged through the canvas covering my head. I steeled myself for blows, either from fists or a blunt object, yet none came. Instead I was thrown roughly to the ground, and was struck by a hard object which bounced off of my chest. Faintly, I heard footsteps running away.

Since my hands had not been bound, I was able to tear off the sack covering my head. I was now in a filthy alleyway, unhurt except for an aching right knee, which had taken the brunt of my fall. "Show yourselves, you cowards!" I shouted, but they were long gone. I looked around for clues but saw none, except for an object lying on the ground near my feet. It was a Philadelphia Deringer, a firearm whose kind I had seen only once. I assumed that this was the hard object that had been thrown at my chest. But to what end?

Pocketing the tiny pistol, I collected my wits enough to examine whether my pocketbook was still in my possession, and to my surprise, found that it was. Whatever my assailants' motive had been, it was not robbery.

Some dangerous drama was playing itself out in the city of Baltimore, and I was determined to discover its nature.

My knee ached terribly the next morning when I arrived at the office, but I said nothing of my assault from the night before, or my failure to identify my attackers, not wishing to hand Hadley and Curlowe more ammunition for ridicule. With Mr. Bellwether's tacit acquiescence I managed to get away from my menial assignments long enough to make my way to the Washington College Hospital, where Edgar Allan Poe drew his final breath, in hopes of finding Dr. John J. Moran. I was told that Dr. Moran was not at present in the city; his personal stock had risen so greatly from becoming known as the physician of the late Poe that he had actually taken to the lecture circuit to give talks about the poet's final hours. Upon further inquiry, I was directed to one Abigail Hewson, who had nursed Poe during his stay at the hospital.

Nurse Hewson was somewhat past middle-years and had a patient, pleasant manner. She well recalled Edgar Allan Poe's days in the hospital, despite the passage of time. "He was not the sort of man one soon forgets," she told me. "The poor fellow was delirious toward the end, but I do not believe it was from alcohol."

"Yet he was in the drink ward," I said.

"Indeed he was, because his symptoms appeared to be drunkenness. But I have seen many unfortunates who have suffered from severe alcoholic poisoning, and in each case their affliction is betrayed by their eyes. They become lifeless, like the eyes of a badly painted portrait. There was no such absence of focus with Mr. Poe, whose eyes were the most penetrating I have ever seen. He looked on me as though he was imploring me to help him."

"Were you present when he cried out for someone named Reynolds?"

"I heard him call out, but it was not 'Reynolds' that Mr. Poe cried, it was *restial*. Do you know what restial is?"

I confessed that I did not.

"It is the request to be buried in the churchyard at no charge and to have the bell toll for one's passing. The poor man knew he was dying. It was obvious from his appearance that he was a pauper, yet he seemed desperate that his body be placed in consecrated ground, like something terrible would happen to his soul otherwise."

I shook my head. "No wonder his last words were 'Lord, help my poor soul.'"

"That is what Dr. Moran remembers," Nurse Hewson said, "but I recall his words differently. Mr. Poe said, *Father*...'Father, help my poor soul'...though I suppose it is all one, when referring to the Almighty."

If, indeed it was the Almighty to which the doomed writer was referring. I now believed he was speaking of his actual, earthly father. I left the hospital with the knowledge that it was imperative that I find the old man again, but how?

Once back at the agency, Old Sam called me into his office. "While you were gallivanting about, a message was delivered for you," he said, handing over an envelope. Opening it, I found a note from Tom Macgowan. *That fellow you've been looking for*, it read, *I believe I have found him. See me when you get this.*

"Mr. Bellwether, I know I have only just arrived back," I said, "but might I go out again?"

Old Sam sighed and threw his hands up in the air in a demonstration of annoyance, but he said: "I suppose emptying the cuspidor can wait. Go on, chase your nonesuch."

I raced to the offices of the *American and Commercial Advisor* and found Tom waiting at the front of the building. "You have seen old Poe?" I asked him.

"I have seen someone I believe to be him," he replied. "I will need you to tell me if I am correct."

"Where is he, then?"

Tom regarded me with a sober expression and then said: "In the city morgue. Come."

Upon arriving at the plain brick building that housed the city's repository of death, Tom showed his press identification to the attendant and we were taken into a foreboding basement room in which several bodies lay on tables, covered by white sheets. We were led to one in particular, whose face was revealed to us. "The body was discovered in an alley," Tom said. "That is him, isn't it?"

I said nothing. While it resembled the man I had met in the tavern, the pallor of death had rendered the once-expressive face so still and stone-like that I could not be certain from his face alone. "Let me see his left hand."

The attendant lifted the sheet at the man's side to reveal the hand, which contained only two fingers. "It is he."

"I suspected as much," Tom said, handing me a battered copy of a booklet titled *Tammerlane and Other Poems by A Bostonian.* "This was found on his person. Read the inscription."

Turning to the booklet's title page I saw an ink scrawl, which I was able to make out as: *To Father, with belated affection; Edgar.* "So he carried this with him to the very moment he finally drank himself to death," I said.

"This fellow did not drink himself to death," the morgue attendant said in a reedy voice. He lowered the sheet down further and revealed a small round bullet hole in the old man's chest.

"Good lord," I uttered. So Mr. Poe's enemies had finally caught up with him.

"The bullet went straight into his heart," the attendant went on. It is a small caliber, too. It must have come from one of those new pistols that one can conceal in a vest pocket."

I suddenly grew cold. "You mean a Philadelphia Deringer?" I heard myself asking.

"Yes, that's what they're called, Deringers. From the size of the hole, I would say that is precisely what this man was shot with."

That evening in my room, I examined the gun that had been tossed into my possession. While I could not prove that it was the same weapon that had killed David Poe, I suspected that to be the truth, just as I suspected that the man's body had been left in a public place because the killer *wanted* it to be discovered. There was a conspiracy of some sort going on, and the decision to saddle me with the pocket pistol was a key part of it. But what in heaven's name was it?

The first peel of eleven sounded from a nearby church tower, and I prepared for bed, hoping the following day might freshen my mind sufficiently to take on the mystery anew. I had no sooner blown out the candles and crawled between the sheets when I heard a commotion outside in the hallway, followed by a forceful knock and the cry: "Police! Open up!"

My instinct was to conceal the Deringer under the mattress before opening the door, but I quickly realized that, were it to be found, I would appear guilty of concealment, and therefore the object of suspicion. Instead I relit the candle and went to the door to open it before the police broke through. A burly police sergeant burst into the room; behind him were three other officers, two of them wielding truncheons and one carrying a lantern. The sergeant demanded my name, which I gave him. "Please tell me what this is about," I demanded in return.

"It's about a dead man in the morgue," the sergeant said. "Someone you knew, according to the attendant."

"I met the man, yes. In fact, I identified him."

One of the officers was now staring at the table and its contents. "Sergeant Broughton, look at this," he said, pointing to the Philadelphia Deringer.

"Mm-hmmm. Is that what you used to kill him?"

"I did not kill anyone," I said. "However, I believe that pistol to be the one that caused his death. It was planted on me to fabricate an illusion of guilt."

"Really."

"Yes, sergeant, really. I have been investigating the circumstances of the man whose body lies in the morgue. If you need verification of my actions, speak with Tom Macgowan of the *American and Commercial Advisor*."

"Were you with Tom Macgowan earlier this evening?"

"Yes, we were at the morgue."

"That's very interesting."

"I detect a note of disbelief in your voice, sergeant. If you do not believe me, then by all means, go speak with Tom."

"That will be a bit difficult, since Mr. Macgowan is the reason we are here. It is *his* body lying in the morgue with a bullet through its middle."

I was too overcome with shock at the news of Tom's murder to resist being restrained and transported to the city jail in Biddle Street. The cell in which I was placed was dark and miserably uncomfortable, and my only company was a snoring sot in the adjoining cell. I demanded that the sergeant notify Samuel Bellwether of my predicament, and then spent a night of fitful rest, desperate in the hopes that Old Sam might come to my rescue. I must have slept some, since I experienced awakening in the cell the next morning. After consuming a loathsome breakfast of gruel and bread, I was told I had visitors. Hopeful that Mr. Bellwether would be one of them, I was unable to conceal my distress when Hadley and Curlowe appeared.

"Nice cage, little birdy," Curlowe sneered. "You know, Jed, I think we've underestimated the pup here. He's come up with a con for the books."

"What are you talking about?" I said, fighting to stave off a headache.

"You came running into Old Sam's office pretending that you'd stumbled over a murder case, when you were really the murderer the whole time."

"That's a lie."

"So what's the story, puppy? You think you can prove you're a real man by going out and killing someone, like they teach you at West Point Finishing School for Young Ladies?"

Headache or not, I charged the bars of my cel and thrust my hand through, hoping to grasp Curlowe's miserable neck, but he managed to step aside with surprising agility. Beside him, Hadley grinned. "You struck a nerve there, Pete," he said. "Junior here needed to prove how tough he was, but he had to find some old, wrecked, one-handed rummy who couldn't fight back to do it. Then his friend at the newspaper found out and he had to kill him, too."

"How is it you seem to know so much about this case?" I asked.

"All we know is what our friends upstairs have told us," Curlowe said. "Or did you even realize that the force here in town and Jed and I are still like that?" He clasped his ham-like hands together in what appeared to be a secret handshake.

"Forget it, Pete," Hadley said. "We've wasted enough time here. All we wanted to do was by and say goodbye, junior. We'll be sure to come to your hanging."

The two of them left, and I seated myself on the cell's filthy cot. Clearly I was not going to be released any time soon, so I set about filling my incarceration time by striving to puzzle out what was happening around me. The deaths of Edgar and David Poe were explainable if one accepted the old man's theory that people were after him for debts, but why on earth had Tom Macgowan been killed? Moreover, why was I being set up for his murder?

After a half-hour of rumination I had achieved little save for a severe throbbing of the temples. It was then that I heard voices and footsteps coming toward the cell. Sergeant Broughton came into view first, and to my great relief, I saw that he was being accompanied by Samuel Bellwether! "Sir!" I cried, rising. "Thank you for coming!"

"Five minutes," the sergeant said, and then lumbered back out.

Old Sam sighed and threw up his hands. "You don't do anything half-way, do you?" he asked.

"You have to believe that I am innocent, Mr. Bellwether."

"Oh, I'm not doubting that, but you have managed to get yourself into a pretty thick jam. You have any idea what you're going to do about it?"

"All I can state with any certainty is that I know what I am *not* going to do, which is be available to fetch your growlers of ale. You will have to send Hadley or Curlowe instead."

"That'll be the day," Old Sam said. "Hadley's father died of drink so he'd like to see every saloon closed and every sot run out of town. As for Curlowe, he stays out of saloons out of deference to Jed, but if he were to go back inside one, all of Hannibal's elephants couldn't drag him back out. If I want an afternoon drink, I'll have to start going back for it myself. As for your problem, son,

I know a lawyer fellow who's pretty cagey. Had a client once who was charged with murder, and got him off without even though he'd been caught red-handed. Let me contact him for you."

Sergeant Broughton eventually returned to announce that the five minute consultation was over. I thanked Mr. Bellwether profusely and watched him leave.

I lay back down on the cot in the cell and closed my eyes, hoping it would ease my persistent headache, and actually began to drift off to sleep. Then my eyes flashed open as a realization penetrated my brain. "Great heavens, could it be?" I asked the cell walls. "Could it really be?" Leaping for the bars, I cried: "Sergeant!" After several such cries, Broughton appeared, with an officer in tow.

"What the matter with you now?"

"Sergeant, I believe I know who killed old Mr. Poe."

"I believe I do, too, and you'd save us a lot of trouble if you'd just confess."

Ignoring his comment, I explained to him what I now believed to be the truth behind the murders of David Poe, his unfortunate son, and probably Tom Macgowan as well. Clearly Broughton was receiving the theory with skepticism, but I had one important question to ask him. I put it to him and his response chased away any doubt in my mind as to the identity of the killer. Finally he said: "You do understand that the man you are accusing of these killings is someone I've known for quite a while, don't you?"

"Are you duty bound to arrest only strangers?" I asked.

Sergeant Broughton scratched his head. "Well, I suppose I could go talk to him."

"I have a better idea," I said, once more explaining myself, and anticipating the policeman's cry of protest. It took another ten minutes of arguing, but finally Sergeant Broughton agreed to let me test my theory. "I'll let you out," he said, unlocking the door, "but I'll have a man on you. If you even think about fleeing you will regret it."

"Upon my honor, sergeant, I will not flee."

I had no reason to flee. But I did need to get word to the Bellwether Detective Agency that I had been released, which Sergeant Broughton agreed to facilitate. He also agreed to see that a letter I was hastily writing was delivered to a particular person; in it I asked the recipient to meet me at seven o'clock at Clancy's Chop

House, an establishment in which I occasionally took my dinner, which was a street down from the Town Crier. Then I went home to wait until the assigned time.

Alas, patience has never been my strongest characteristic.

When I grew tired of pacing in my room I decided to go to the restaurant before the appointed time. I took my time walking there so that the policeman I knew was tailing me was never in doubt as to my intentions. Once at Clancy's I took a corner table and ordered a coffee, and sat back to watch the door, waiting for my quarry.

Seven o'clock came and went, and my invited guest did not appear. Had I been foolish, thinking I could summon a killer into a public place? Or had he simply not received the letter? Or was I completely wrong in my the realization I had made from Samuel Bellwether casual comment?

By eight o'clock, I was forced to accept the truth that my plan had failed. I rose from my table and headed back to my rooming house.

It was nearly dark when I arrived there. I dragged myself up the stairs and opened the door to my room, not even bothering to light the candle on the table. I knew the room well enough to navigate it in the dark. Removing my jacket and throwing it into a chair, I walked to the bed and stretched out on it, and ruminated about my future as a detective; nay, my future in general.

From somewhere in the darkened room, I heard the click of a pistol hammer. Bolting upright, I now saw a dark shadow standing against the window, barely discernable against the dying light of day. "Who is there?" I called out.

"The man you sent for," a voice replied. The figure struck a match and touched it to the wick of the candle. In the dim glow I could see the barrel of the pocket pistol that was trained at me. "If you knew the first thing about detective work, you would know that only an idiot would walk into an obvious trap like the one you tried to set for me. I decided to meet you here instead."

"How did you get in here?"

"A real detective wouldn't have to ask that, either. Breaking and entering is an occasional aspect of the job."

"What are you going to do with me?"

"I am going to witness your spoken confession, which will be followed by your anguished self-destruction—a bullet through the brain—which I will be powerless to prevent."

"Do not think staging my suicide will go easy."

"Easy or hard, it is only the end result that matters."

"I've already told everything I know to the police."

"You mean Broughton? My old chum when I was on the force? Once I have convinced him that you set out to incriminate me, to the point of making your desperate suicide look like it was done by my hand, he'll beg my forgiveness for ever listening to you. But out of curiosity, just what did you tell Broughton?"

"I told him that you are responsible for the deaths of Edgar Allan Poe, David Poe, and Tom Macgowan. Both the old man and Tom you shot through the heart, though in the case of Edgar I have to assume you used some sort of poison which left him raving and delirious. Moreover, I believe that you assaulted me on the street, with the help of another, and planted the murder weapon on me, at least the one used on David Poe. The pistol in your hand I presume to be the one you used to murder Tom."

"And why do you *presume* I did all this?"

"You killed Edgar Poe because you thought he was David Poe. Edgar was wearing his father's clothes, and you simply mistook him for his father. Once old Mr. Poe realized that he was the intended victim, he must have gone into hiding. Once he emerged, you found him and killed him, too. As for Tom, I can only assume that his investigation into the case began to reveal facts that you did not want brought to light."

"A fanciful story, but one that completely unravels unless you can explain why I would want to kill the old man in the first place."

"Because he was a drunk, like your father."

Even in the dimness I could see Jed Hadley's face harden.

"Old Sam told me of your hatred of drink," I went on. "Was killing a sot like David Poe your way of killing your memory of your father?"

There was a moment of silence, followed by a sound that disturbed me more than any I was prepared hear: uncontrollable laughter. Once he regained his composure, Hadley said: "My God, I had you pegged as an imbecilic tin soldier, but this is richer than anything I could imagine! I'll admit it was particularly satisfying to be able to rid the world of a useless tosspot, but that was not why I set after the old wretch."

"Why then?"

"Because I was *paid* to, junior," Hadley said. "You see, I offer a special service that even old Bellwether knows nothing about. For the right price, I will eliminate anyone, for any reason. I was contacted by a man to whom Prince, or Poe, owed a sizable gambling debt. He knew he would never see his money, so he settled for revenge. I followed the man I believed to be my quarry and treated him to a bottle of good gin. He was in such a celebratory mood that he did not notice the smell of the formaldehyde."

"Good lord," I muttered.

"My error became clear a few days later, and my employer was not happy about my mistake. It took all of my persuasive powers to keep from becoming his next target, by I managed, with the promise that I would keep looking for the intended victim, which I did for over a year before concluding that he was already dead. My employer accepted my judgment, though I was unable to collect my fee for killing the wrong man. Then like manna from the heavens, you come walking into the agency and announce that you have found the father of Edgar Allan Poe! I pretended not to believe you, but I knew you were telling the truth. You have no idea what a gift you were. I was offered one more chance to kill my quarry and finally collect my fee, and since you were already looking for the man, you would become the perfect suspect for a murder investigation. That, however, would require an unambiguous murder, so I abandoned the formaldehyde and used a simple firearm instead. All I had to do was to shoot the sodden old fool and then saddle you with the gun."

"But Tom Macgowan figured out what you were doing, so he had to die, too."

"True, although up until the point at which his suspicions became dangerous, he played his part admirably."

"What are you talking about?"

"It was Macgowan who helped me rough you up," Hadley said.

"*What*? I cannot believe that!"

Hadley chuckled. "After you mentioned your friend at the *Advisor*, I went to see him. I learned a little bit more about the two of you, particularly about how you used to pull pranks on each other at the Academy. So I laid out a little proposition: how would he like to assist me in a prank that would test your mettle as an operative, in return for my feeding him information on future cases? I promised him I wouldn't really hurt you, so he agreed, and we tossed you around that night. But when the old man's body turned up, he began to make connections that were, shall we say, troublesome for me. Occasionally the situation necessitates plying my trade without compensation."

"You cannot get away with all these murders," I said. "Others will make the same connections. Eventually you will be caught."

"There are other towns with a need for a good operative who offers special services," he rejoined. "If too many questions arise, I will leave and start over elsewhere. But for the moment, I need something from you."

"From me? What?"

"Macgowan was a clever sort so I was not surprised when he began to piece things together. You, however, are a feeble-brained cadet. Yet something I did planted the seed of suspicion in you. Tell me what it was so I know not to repeat it."

"It was actually something Mr. Bellwether said at the jail. He was speaking of a lawyer who won freedom for a client who had been caught red-handed. That brought to mind the image of Mr. Poe's ruined hand, which was scarred and red. Then something you said earlier, when you were taunting me in the jail, jumped into my head. You referred to David Poe as a 'one-handed rummy.' I knew that Mr. Poe had only one good hand, because he showed it to me. Later, Tom saw it in the morgue. When I questioned Sergeant Broughton about it, though, he had no knowledge of the man's ruined hand."

"So what?"

"Curlowe stated that everything the two of you knew about these murders came from your friends in the police, yet they knew nothing of the damaged hand. So how did you know? You had to have gotten close enough to David Poe to see his hand. That was an inconsistency in your story."

"Which in no way proves I killed him."

"You have already admitted to killing him. All that I required was the chance to confront you with the inconsistency, and trust that you would do the rest, which you did."

Hadley sighed. "Well, well, well, so there is a working brain in that vapid head after all." Then he slowly stepped toward me and pressed the cold barrel of the Deringer against my left temple. "It will not, however, work for much longer."

I was seated on my bed with a gun pointed directly to my head. I knew if I moved I would probably be shot before I could take a step. However, if I remained still, I would definitely be shot.

I opted to move.

Lunging forward as rapidly as I could, I dove for the chair and grabbed my jacket, which lay over the top of it, and swung it at the candle, which fell over and extinguished. I then spun around while continued to swing the garment as forcefully as I could until it connected with Jed Hadley's arm, forcing it downward as the pistol fired, lodging its bullet into the floor. I turned and bolted out of the room and down the stairs as fast as my legs would propel me, expecting at any moment to be felled by another bullet.

Luckily, it never came. I made it to the front door of the boarding house and burst through it, only to hear a familiar cry: "Hey, son!" Standing in front of the house were Samuel Bellwether, Sergeant Broughton and two armed officers!

A moment later Hadley came through the door, pistol still in his hand, though four guns were trained on him before he was able to reach the porch steps. "You can't win this one, Jed," Mr. Bellwether called. "Drop the pistol."

Hadley did as instructed and the policemen rushed him, binding his hands behind him and dragging him off the porch. As he passed us, I could hear him trying to persuade Sergeant Broughton that this was a misunderstanding, and that the real killer was getting away. To his credit, the sergeant was having none of it.

Mr. Bellwether asked me to join him at the Town Crier, and I readily agreed. If ever I needed a drink to calm my nerves, it was now. As we walked to the tavern, I said: "You have no idea how glad I was to see you and the police, but how did you know I was in trouble?"

"Sergeant Broughton called me down to the station and explained your theory about Hadley," he said. "I confess that I had a hard time believing that one of my men could be a murderer. But when I got back, I watched Hadley closely for the rest of the day. In particular I noticed a change in his usual demeanor when he received that note you sent to him. When Hadley left for the day, I told Curlowe to tail him. He didn't like it, but I'm his boss, so he did it. He tailed him right to your house. By that point even Pete realized that something was going on that wasn't on the level, and came back to report. I went to get the police. I'm just glad we got there in time."

"So am I, Mr. Bellwether."

Old Sam's face suddenly appeared to take on both age and weariness. Godamighty," he sighed, "a cold-blooded killer working right under my nose, in my own office, and I don't even know it. Some detective I am."

If Tom Macgowan were alive, he might have written that Jed Hadley's arrest shook the city of Baltimore to its very core. Upon searching Hadley's home for evidence, the police discovered a hidden file containing the names of all of his secret clients, and information relating to a series of murders he had accomplished on their behalf. On a more personal level, Old Sam Bellwether wasted little time in making me a full operative with my own case load and ordered Pete Curlowe to either accept the new situation or move elsewhere. He chose to move elsewhere. The last I heard Curlowe was once again in uniform, back in the force over in Washington D.C.

The hot summer of 1852 quickly gave way to a cool autumn. On the seventh day of October of that year, having finished work on a particularly challenging robbery case, I stopped into the Town Crier for a beer. A host of conflicting emotions flooded over me as I sat at the bar in the place where I had earlier connected with two gentlemen, both of whom were now gone. It was only after I had paid my tab and prepared to leave that the significance of the day's date dawned on me. Going back to the bar I ordered a small bottle of cognac and took it with me.

Walking to the Westminster Hall and Burying Ground in Fayette Street, I entered the grounds and found the stone I was looking for, the one inscribed with the name Edgar Allan Poe, who went to his reward exactly three years ago this very day. I left the bottle of cognac in front of his stone and walked on to another grave, an unmarked one located close by. Even though there was no stone, I knew who was buried there. I had paid for the restial myself. Stopping a moment, I fished a silver dollar out of my pocket. "You were the gambler, sir," I said to the ground, and then flipped the coin into the air and caught it again, slapping it onto the back of my left hand. "Call it, Mr. Poe." I lifted my right hand and saw the side upon which it had landed. "You win," I said, smiling.

I tossed the coin into the grave and strode on.

✗

"First off I'd like to address the rumor that I'm not really running things around here."

THE DOUBLE

by Janice Law

Mostly when I have a problem here, I consult with Evelyn, who's done so much to smooth my way in this strange land, but not this time. There's no way she could help me with the General.

For starters, how could I ever explain General Rezart to her? Sure, she's seen him on TV; she reads the papers, but words alone cannot convey the impact of the General, a truly remarkable man—and remarkably far-sighted. His foresight, as well as his psychopathic tendencies, were the difference between him and the rest of us. But while his violence and cruelty became public, even international, knowledge, his visionary grasp of future contingencies remained private. I think I'm first to understand just how far ahead the General planned.

We'd been thrown together in the old Red army, where Rezart was a corporal and I was his sergeant. Our resemblance was so marked that some joker suggested we trade places and see whether Lieutenant Dragusha would notice. I forgot that incident; the General-To-Be remembered.

Came the collapse of the Communist empire, old Royalists and nationalist fanatics joined former Reds and spanking new capitalists. While most hesitated, uncertain which banner would be safest, the General-To-Be acted, as you know. If you don't, the history of our sad country will enlighten you. I was demobilized by that time, running a building supply yard in a border province, living an ordinary life, half considering marriage, hoping for opportunity, and keeping my head down politically. Surviving, in short, the way we did in those days.

I'd still be there, in sight of the great pass and the unmelting snows with eagles overhead in blue mountain air, if a black Mercedes hadn't arrived late one afternoon, lumbering out of the dust, the low red sun reflecting on the windshield. Three men in city suits got out; I knew they weren't interested in building lumber or cement blocks or a few pounds of nails.

I figured that I'd been denounced, that a little business I'd done across the border had attracted notice, that I had an enemy. I actually considered mentioning the General, something along the lines of, "You realize I was in the same regiment as the General, Beloved of Us All," but these boys were so efficient, I didn't even get my mouth open.

"You have an opportunity to serve the state and the General," they announced and bundled me into the car. The Mercedes wallowed across the potholes in the dirt road, later to be paved by the General's fiat, and between my dusty provincial shop and the port, the center of the General's power, they made their proposal.

The General had remembered me, not for my many good qualities, my exceptional intelligence and stalwart friendship, but for the shape of my nose, the breadth of my shoulders, the unusual length of my arms. He had many enemies, some desperate; he needed a double. I was his man.

One of several, in fact, but within months, I was unquestionably the mainstay. As the General, I met boring ambassadors, inaugurated public works in unsettled areas, ate at banquets with gunmen and fanatics. I was a quick study, and I was good. Lacking the ruthlessness to become a General on my own, I nonetheless discovered some of the qualities needed to *be* the General. After I survived a second assassination attempt, I dared to improvise remarks from the door of the ambulance—if the tape has survived in the archives, you can judge my performance for yourself.

Immediately after I was discharged from the hospital, I was summoned to see my former military comrade at the palace, a structure dating from the old monarchy: marble turrets, glorious tiled roofs and walls, acres of gardens with date palms, exotic birds, and flowers of all kinds. Beautiful, of course, but I was shaking.

Thanks to the nasty scar under my collarbone and a stiff shoulder, I was no longer so exact a double, and, knowing the General's paranoia and the reputation of his secret police, I was afraid that a quick shot in the head was probably the best of my prospects.

But as he would so often, the devious General surprised me. "You saved my life, Malik," he said, stepping forward on the gleaming floor and kissing me on both cheeks, "as was your duty." Then without preliminary, I was ordered to shave my beard, trim my hair, and learn a new language. I was to be sent abroad.

"A position of great trust," said the General, "only to be offered to someone who was a comrade in arms."

I bowed, still barely able to breathe. "And my duties, General?"

He waved his hand. "Make a life, something respectable and comfortable, but

without connections. That's very important, no wife or children. A job? Possibly; the society is said to be industrious, and I want no questions asked about you. You need to fit in, like the glove on my hand."

He smoothed the kid gloves that he wore even indoors, even in what seemed to me stifling heat. Rezart had always been highly sensitive to cold. I saw him turning my life inside out like a skinned rabbit, and I hesitated before his power.

He nodded slightly, as if he appreciated my reservations. He was not then, as he later became, totally blind to the feelings and wishes of others. "The alternative," he said and paused.

I understood that only too well. "It will be an honor to serve you, General," I said.

Rezart kissed me on both cheeks again, and I was dismissed into the custody of the men in the dark suits and cloudy glasses. Study, language coaching, a new name, new documents, new money, and finally a flight to a vastly bigger and richer port city, a hot, bright, glossy, godless place where I have lived comfortably for fifteen years, thanks to the General.

When I get up in the early morning, I step out of the air-conditioned house into the cool of the yard. Doves call in the trees, my parrot squawks, potted orchids bloom along the fence. Tall palms and pines break the sun, which gains an extra glitter from the sea just two blocks away. This is a desirable property, one of several I own and manage. I could live on my rents if the General cuts my stipend—something I have expected for fourteen years, at least.

Perhaps you are granting him the virtue of gratitude? Not me, yet even I did not

anticipate how far ahead he looked. A remarkable man, whatever his faults and vices.

I lived as I'd been instructed. I was watched, of course; that went without saying. I found the heat distasteful initially, but I discovered the beaches and learned to swim; I grew dark in the sun. I invented a past, unnecessarily as it turned out. People came to *this* port city to escape cold, bleakness, and regret; the young for fun, the old for death in comfort. I was among exiles.

I cultivated small vices. I grew lazy and refused work; the apartments were enough. I had no wife—a curious stipulation—but there seemed to be no objection to women, "girlfriends" was the local term, or to boozy nights dancing at clubs or afternoons sunning at the "clothing optional" beach; the General was an eccentric, not a puritan.

Periodically, I was "refreshed" with tapes from home, recordings of the General, both video and audio, brought via the diplomatic bag, a useless skullduggery now that my satellite dish brings forth, in somewhat dark and grainy video, the official station of my homeland. Lately I've been able to see the Republic Day Parade, the birthday celebrations of the General, Beloved of Us All, and his annual visit to the Tomb of the Fallen. He looked older, as if unlimited power were beginning to tell on him.

Predictable. There have been the usual troubles in the mountains, my home province, plus difficulties with miners in the south, and with intellectuals in the port city, his base. While I'd been relaxing, enjoying life, and learning curious things from Evelyn, he was fighting and executing and watching his back.

I don't know if he anticipated the coup that finally ended his rule, but when it came he acted with his usual dispatch. According to the various accounts, the General disappeared by plane, by boat, by mule over the mountain passes. His flight was on the news along with glimpses of bearded men, myself in youth, waving kalashnikovs and dancing in the streets, anticipating good times that would never arrive.

I felt mostly relief; no more cash but no more surveillance, either. I could move, if I liked, to the mountains, which I had not allowed myself to miss; I might even go home. Those were my thoughts, but just when it seemed that the General had left my life, Albert visited my house.

He'd had another name originally, dropped along with the euphonious vowels and plentiful consonants of our native tongue. Now he wore the local garb of bright printed shirts, shorts, and sandals. The only remnant of his former attire were his dark glasses—"shades" is the suggestive local term—and he was wearing them as he stood on my doorstep in the quickening tropical darkness.

"You have an opportunity to serve the state and the General, Beloved of Us All," he said by way of greeting.

I waved him inside. "The capitol has fallen, and the General is probably dead," I said, but my mind had already lurched into high gear.

"Don't you believe it," said Albert. Then, drawing himself up in way made ridiculous by his beach clothes, he said, "You will be asked to do a great service for Him Who is Beloved of Us All," and added, for like me, he'd been in exile long enough to pick up the distinctive lingo of the place, "Remember, you've been on his dime for years."

He laid out the plan with certain significant omissions which I could fill in all too easily. In brief, The General, Beloved of Us All (and Crafty as Hell) would arrive shortly with a small entourage. "Your house may not be sufficiently large," Albert said disapprovingly.

"Have them stay at a motel," I suggested, for I both believed Albert and didn't believe him at the same time.

Albert frowned. "The General will need some information from you. You will be debriefed."

"And then?" I asked.

"Why the General, Beloved of Us All, will take your place. He will become 'Mal,' who lives on apartment rentals and drinks and dances at The Neon Grove and sees the red-haired Ms. Grabbleston."

This was a threat; I said nothing. Of course, they would have known about Evelyn; I'd just ignored the idea. "No connections," the General had warned me. Now Evelyn would be expendable, even as I was.

"Fifteen years is a long time," Albert said philosophically. Easy for him.

"For you, too," I said. Even Albert must have made "connections," developed habits, formed pleasurable routines.

"I have not the honor to resemble the General," said Albert.

That night I took Evelyn out to dinner, intending to break things off, to give her a running start, so to speak. Instead, I found myself asking her about murder. Our port city is rich in crime, and Evelyn is a writer. She lives off the proceeds of a volume entitled,

Releasing Your Inner Wild Woman, but she's been known to dabble in crime fiction.

"Lots of people get shot here," she said. "With our stupid gun laws."

"Bang. Not very interesting. And then?"

"Then the canals, of course. Bang and splash."

We need to quarrel, I told myself. *We need to quarrel, so Evelyn will be safe,* but I hated the idea, and my hatred was behind my questions. I not only wanted to kill the General, I needed to kill him.

"Coming back for a nightcap?" she asked. "I think the Wild Woman wants out."

As a fan of wild women, particularly wild women as attractive as Evelyn, I decided that we could quarrel later. You can see I'd become lazy and indecisive, for we were still on good terms when she nipped into the shower after a pleasant interlude. I was listening to the water running—a lovely sound if you are from a dry country—and thinking how best to offend her when she called, "Have I got any cigarettes left? They'll be in the bedside table."

I opened the drawer to find, not cigarettes, but a .38 caliber pistol. This was a surprise, although not a huge surprise. Though a proponent of gun laws, Evelyn lives in what the locals call a "transitional" neighborhood. The pistol was her last line of defense and possibly my salvation.

The General won't know about this, I thought. Even Albert and his spies won't know. I stuck the pistol in a pocket and folded my jacket carefully. Then I got dressed. When I kissed Evelyn goodbye at the door, I had her .38 tucked up, fully loaded, in my best silk blazer.

A good beginning, but concealment was a difficulty. The house was out, definitely out. Surely the General would come with professionals. The yard, then, the yard. I could feel my heart beating. The palms, the doves, Serena, my parrot. They'll kill my pretty Serena, too, I thought, and I opened the cage door for her. The orchids blooming—would the General care for them? Fat chance, but they might check the pots. Might. At the corner of the house, the air conditioner hummed softly. It was a big powerful model, which the AC guy came once a year to service. I could see him lifting the top, and I went into the house for some duct tape.

In a few minutes, I had the top off and the gun taped to the underside of the cover. I closed the lid and went into the house to wash my hands. I had a secret that might become a resource.

Early the next morning I woke up. The doves calling in the trees were too familiar a sound to have awakened me. No, it was the rattle of a key turning in the front door; Albert must have availed himself of a copy. Reminding myself of my hidden resource, I went downstairs to meet my old army colleague, Rezart, the General, who looked pale and tired, his famed vigor drained, his face lined.

He wanted whisky, and he wanted to sleep. Although the guest room was ready, he preferred my room, and I changed the sheets for him. Then I sat in the living room while his three bodyguards searched the house, turning over my things and examining, with noticeable envy, the array of consumer goods so readily available in my new home port.

They wanted to know the details of my day, the names of acquaintances, the value of the rents on the apartments. And also my insurance company, regular monthly bills, my bank account numbers. I realized that they would kill me when they knew enough.

My tanned skin presented a problem for them, my speech, too. They had not anticipated that I would be almost perfect in my adopted tongue. I suggested it would be best to sell the apartments and the house and minimize contact with my acquaintances.

They smiled wolfishly as if they guessed that I was trying to delay.

At three p.m., the General came into the living room to demand orange juice, which he drank sitting on the sofa with the wolves on either side. I noticed he had a metal case with him. Documents, I guessed, cash, details of various numbered accounts. The man who would be "Mal" would be rich and able to buy safety.

"So Malik," he said. "So many years and we meet so far away."

"It is always a pleasure to see you, General."

"You have done well," he said. "An obscure life can be a happy one. Though this house is too small, I am pleased. Mostly. There are, of course, details. No one lives without entanglements, do they?"

I could only agree.

"We must cut those off." He made a chopping motion. "You understand."

"This is a large country," I suggested. "We would never need to meet."

The General sighed. "But I believe every individual is unique. There can only be one of you, Malik, and that will now be me. You understand," he said.

I did.

That afternoon, the General shaved off his famous moustache and had one of the guards thin his thick crown of hair. He helped himself to a shirt and a pair of slacks from my closet. "These are a bit tight," he remarked. He applied a quickie-tanning product and checked himself in the mirror. I thought he looked sad; satisfied with his plan, yes, but sad, too.

When the sun went down, the General wished to go for a ride. He wanted to see the historic tourist district, the shore, the rivers, and waterways. I realized that in his career, the General had few chances to play the tourist. The night air was warm, and he said that a ride would do us good. I shrugged, thinking how quickly he worked, how little time I'd been allotted. One of the bodyguards phoned Albert to bring a car. When the phone rang unanswered, I wondered if Albert had taken advantage of his non-nondescript appearance to decamp.

"You can take my car," I suggested. "It will hold three or four comfortably."

"You will drive," said the General. "There must be no irregularities."

We got into the car, the General beside me in the front, two of the guards in the back. The third man was to stay behind and to locate Albert, who had angered the General by his defection. We drove down the main beach route with the restaurants, clubs, and shops on one side, the sand and water on the other. Roller bladers zipped along the sidewalk; motorbikes were noisy on the street; women sauntered in backless dresses and young men with earrings and tattoos stood talking on the corners.

I remarked that the beaches were famous.

"I do not understand putting oneself into salt water," the General said, and I remembered, dimly, that he did not know how to swim. Despite our single, vital port, we are a mountain people.

I need to kill this man, I thought, and *I need to do it quickly. Him and his guards, too, and leave the life I've built behind.* But the .38

was taped to the inside cover of the AC unit in my yard and the General's men were sitting in the back seat.

"There is too much traffic here," the General said.

"From here until the Everglades."

When he said, "Drive west," and he settled himself comfortably in the seat, I knew they were going to kill me.

Why hadn't I brought the .38 with me? Made an excuse to visit the yard or even made a break through the neighborhood? Now there was nothing to stop them. They'd have me pull over on some deserted stretch where, with one quick shot, my edition of Mal would be food for gators.

I gripped the wheel, sweating even in the air conditioning. We had reached the head of Alligator Alley before despair suggested a desperate solution. Even then I drove for several miles in anguished indecision before a dark, empty stretch decided me.

I could see the lights glistening on the black surface of the wide drainage canal that runs along the right hand side of the road. I took a deep breath, floored the accelerator, and wrenched the wheel. We shot from the smooth hum of the tarmac to the bounce and swerve of the grass, our heads thumping the ceiling, before, with a gut dropping lurch, we were in an airborne plunge toward the water. The Toyota hit the surface of the canal with a mighty splash and bobbed into an absolute, disorienting blackness.

Yelling and blows; thrashing and struggling. I unfastened my belt and fumbled desperately for the window. One of the guards was flailing at me and trying to climb into the front seat, and the General, I'm sure it was Rezart, clawed for my throat. I grabbed the handle and opened the window; the canal poured in, producing more frenzy as the water drenched our legs and thighs and rose inexorably chest deep, neck deep, nose deep.

Amazing that I can remember anything at such a moment, but Evelyn, a native of this swampy land, had drilled me on the dangers of canals and the ways to survive them. I took a gulp of air from the diminishing bubble trapped near the ceiling, then, when the pressure equalized, shoved the door open and floundered into the muddy water. A hand clutched my leg. I kicked myself free, but in my frenzied struggle I became disoriented and touched the horror of the bottom muck.

With scarcely any breath left, I twisted and clawed my way through the water, banging into the side of the car. Terrified of re-entering the vehicle in the darkness, I tasted oblivion, before the lessons of our fine municipal pool return to me. I stopped struggling and, magically, began to rise through the alien fluid.

With an astonished gasp, I broke into the sweet air; the soft southern night, jeweled with highway lights, arched above my head. One stroke, two, three, more, quick, quick, floundering on despite the shock, the pain in my ribs, the difficulty of taking breath: The canals have both alligators and snakes. I didn't stop flailing until I reached the bank and clawed myself up through the sharp edged grasses that sliced my fingers.

Struggling for breath, I flopped onto my back, amazed by survival and the continuing thunder of my heart. I was alive, and only a few ripples broke the surface of the canal. Our great national poet was right: We are no more than bubbles in some celestial wine. Already all signs of life and struggle were dissolving; against all odds, I had out-lasted my old military colleague, the General.

I sat up to pour muddy water out of my shoes. The night was warm; my clothes would dry. "I believe every individual is unique," the General had said. He was right; there *is* something unnatural about doubles.

I got a lift at the Miccosukee truck stop and walked several miles of city streets to my house, where I found the living room still bright behind the blinds. The General's faithful guard was keeping watch. In the light of my security spot, another local necessity, I eased off the cover of the air conditioner and retrieved Evelyn's pistol. I regretted that there would be no more sessions with the author of *Releasing Your Inner Wild Woman*; she would have to find a new partner for late evenings at The Neon Grove and early nights to bed.

I unlocked the door and called softly in our native tongue. The guard would believe me, or he would not. If he did not, I would kill him. And perhaps, some remnant of the General whispered, I would kill him even if he did.

"Did you find Albert, that traitor?"

"No, General, with regret, General." Then he hesitated. "Where are..."

"There was an accident. The man, Malik, put up resistance."

He took a step toward the General's case, left for safekeeping. He was reaching into his jacket pocket when I raised Evelyn's .38 and shot him dead on the pale rug.

I went through to the bedroom to change my clothes. Four men were dead and my pleasant life was a shambles, but I felt curiously indifferent. The General believed that each individual is unique. He said there could only be one Malik, alias Mal, and he intended to be the one. But he was wrong. There was only one Rezart, one psychopathic, far-sighted, Beloved of Us All and Crafty as Hell General, and I was he. I'd trained for twenty years for his life, and now I was destined to be the General, killer and fugitive, forever.

✗

THE WAY IT IS

by Carole Buggé

You lie on your bed late at night listening to the swoosh of passing cars in the rain on the street outside. There's a round, rumbling sound as they roll over the manhole cover in front of the building, a double, one-*two* percussion as the wheels pass over the metal cover, first the front and then the back wheels. It's a friendly sound, like a hollow drum, and it keeps you company as you stare at the tiny silver stars swirling around in your lava lamp. You imagine each star as a lost soul, caught up in the hot liquid of the lamp, forever circling around each other. The stars are swimming in their purple lava bath, the cars are plowing through a February thunderstorm, but you are warm and dry on your bed, covered with the quilt your mother gave you for Christmas. You lie listening to the raindrops hitting the air conditioner. You see the words the sounds spell out in your head: *plunck, plop, thrrat, rat-a-thwop plat.*

You're always happier when it's raining, especially at night when you don't have to go out and you can lie on top of your bed with your mother's quilt wrapped around your knees. It's a comfort, the rain, and you begin to imagine what would happen if it never stopped raining, if the water from the East River began to rise until it flooded its banks and everyone would have to move to higher ground.

Move to higher ground.

There is no higher in New York — downtown, where you live, is flat as a skillet. The water would just spread over everything until the city was under water. It's what happened in New Orleans, but New York has never suffered from a natural disaster like Hurricane Katrina, only man made disasters.

What rained out of the sky that day was death death in the form of religious fanaticism. You've had your bout with mysticism, and you're still not sure that trees don't have spirits, but you have trouble understanding the allure of organized religion.

But there it was that day, swooping down like a big, ugly bird of prey, suddenly swallowing the southern tip of the island You've tried:

Talking it out.

Crying it out.

Swallowing it and moving on.

But what you can't stop is the image of your sister, arriving with the rest of the catering staff, so excited, so happy to be working at Windows on the World. You remember the phone call the night before:

"How are you going to fix your hair?"

"I don't know, Kelley, I haven't thought about it."

You tried not to dampen her enthusiasm, but you never had her keen spirit. You were the sensible one, the quiet one, but she was the one people looked at when she entered rooms — even though you were identical twins, it was always her shining, eager face that drew stares.

"I'm going to put mine in French braids. I think that will be elegant but it

will keep it out of my face."

French braids. Her snow-blond hair, wrapped around itself in a coil like strands of DNA endlessly repeating bits of information, genetic codes that mapped out the existence of a human being, a single organism. And now these strands exist only in you — but you feel not so much like a human being as leftover matter, like the tail of a comet that has passed on into another star system.

You were supposed to be there; you had your clothes all carefully laid out the night before, but you awoke in the night with the flu, with chills and vomiting that shook your body and left you breathless and sweating. It seems like such a crummy excuse now, though, and you are left with the feeling that you should have been there. But this is the way it is: you weren't there.

Kelley was there, though, no doubt on time as usual, bouncy and bright in her starched white chef's coat. What she wanted from life was so simple: to cook for people, to make and serve them well prepared, healthy food. What was so unreasonable about that — why, you wonder, was it too much to ask to make a life out of nourishing people? She planned to open her own restaurant someday — a small, intimate place with good prices and even better food.

You would work for her — you were always more comfortable in your position as second fiddle, and she was always so gracious, so grateful to you for your devotion.

A car passes by outside, hitting a large puddle and splashing rain water onto the sidewalk. You imagine a pedestrian jumping out of the way, like a Laurel and Hardy movie. Except that Stan Laurel eventually would end up pushing Oliver Hardy into the puddle by mistake, then, feeling bad about it, would whimper in that high-pitched whine of his until a sputtering Hardy forgave him.

Forgiveness.

Your last shrink was a Buddhist and encouraged you to forgive — forgive yourself, forgive others, and ask others for forgiveness. Good advice, except that how could you ask Kelley, when she isn't here anymore? *Please forgive me for not dying with you, Kelley.*

You've tried saying it to her departed spirit, but you don't really believe in life after death, so it never feels like anyone is listening.

You glance over at the matte knife on the bedside table, its blade reflecting silver in the glow of the lava lamp like the gleaming silver planes that rained down on the city that day. In books and movies people always use razor blades, but a matte knife is so much easier to handle. You imagine sinking into the warm water in the bathtub, letting it cover your body. It will only sting for a moment, you think, and then a long slow slide into unconsciousness.

And then you will be with Kelley.

A HOUSE DIVIDED

by Marc Bilgrey

It was a sunny afternoon in late March, 1865. My company had been on its way to Richmond when we were ambushed. I ran for cover in the nearby woods hoping to circle around the Rebs and take them from the opposite direction. I thought I might bring down an officer or two in the process. But no sooner had I entered the dense foliage when I was met by a gray who butted me in the head with his rifle. Then I dropped to the ground like a marble statue. After that everything went black.

When I awoke hours later, I clutched my aching head and looked up to discover a full moon shining in a dark sky. Around me were the bodies of both Union and Confederate men. I can only suppose that both sides had left me for dead.

As I gazed upon this macabre sight I thought about what a grim business it all was. I had agreed to serve my government to the best of my abilities, for I am not a coward. But, just the same, I took no particular joy in it either.

Staggering to my feet I discovered that my Colt .32 caliber revolver, Enfield .57 caliber rifle, knapsack, haversack, belt and cartridge box were gone. Looted no doubt. After looking in vain for a canteen amongst the corpses I made my way through the trees till I came to a clearing. There I hoped to find a drink of water.

"Good evening, Billy Yank," said a voice.

Instinctively I reached for my gun but found nothing, not even a holster. I spun around to see a Reb staring me in the face. His gray uniform was ripped in the right arm and he had dried blood on his upper lip. He looked to be even younger than I, which was twenty. The tiny bugle insignia on his kepi told me he was infantry, same as me. I saw him aim his smoothbore musket straight at my chest.

"Good evening, Johnny Reb," I said. Without my gun I knew my options were extremely limited.

He came closer. As he did, I heard a cannon blast in the far distance. For a split second he turned toward it. This brief lapse of attention allowed me the time to leap upon him.

He fought fiercely as we wrestled about in the dirt like two dogs fighting over a bone. He was able to land a blow to my stomach. Recovering quickly, I sent an uppercut to his chin, dazing him enough so that I was able to pry the musket out of his hands. I turned the barrel to his head as my finger found the trigger.

"Drop your gun, Yankee!" yelled a voice behind me. "Drop it or I kill you!"

I let the musket fall from my hands to the ground.

"Stand up now!" said the man's voice. "The both of you and I ain't got all day."

The Reb and I stood up. As we did we looked at the man who was giving us the orders. He was wearing a pair of brown trousers, boots and a green shirt. He had a long white beard and in his right hand was a C.S. Spiller and Burr .36 caliber revolver.

"Now," he said, addressing us, "step away from the musket."

When we had taken a few steps back, the old man came over, still holding the revolver and staring us down, reached over and picked up the Reb's musket. Then to my amazement, he smashed the musket against some rocks and threw the pieces off into the woods.

"I don't understand," said the Reb, "why are you doing this? We're on Confederate soil. You ought to be helping me take this here Yankee to his just reward, not—"

"I'll thank you to not be giving me any advice, soldier," said the old man, moving his gun just slightly toward the Reb. "Didn't anyone ever tell you to show a little respect 'round your elders?" The old man pursed his lips and said, "Okay boys, here's how it's gonna be. You listen to me and do exactly as I say or I will put some very large holes in you. Nod if you understand me."

I nodded. I was too scared to even look toward the Reb. Being taken prisoner by the enemy was one thing but what this man had in mind, only the fates knew for certain.

"All right, fellas," said the old man, "now y'all gonna turn around and start walking. You will walk up to that there ridge and then you will continue to walk till I tell you to stop. And keep in mind that I have the firearm and I ain't afraid to use it. In point of fact, I would be more than glad to use it. It don't matter to me which one of you boys tries anything in the way of an escape attempt. I will kill you where you stand same as I would kill a squirrel for my dinner. Or if you both give it a try, so much the better. I could use the target practice. Not that I need it. I been known to bag a songbird at one hundred paces. Now then, let's start marching."

We began walking. The Reb was next to me. Neither of us said a word. Behind us I heard the old man's footfalls in the twigs. We passed trees and bushes and not much else. I wondered where this old man was taking us. Was it some kind of Rebel trick? Perhaps they were working together and planned to torture me for the purpose of extracting information. I hoped not, since I didn't know a blessed thing. I was a private, not a general.

Here I was, six months into my conscription and thus far luck or providence had prevailed. Though I had seen battle, other than a few minor cuts, I had emerged unscathed. But now I was convinced all was lost.

I was suddenly seized by a severe bout of homesickness. It occurred to me that I would never again witness another sunrise over the Hudson River nor picnic in the bucolic hills of the Bronx with my parents and sisters. The thought of no longer being able to stop in front of Van Horn's Dry Goods Shop, look in the window and see my father working behind the counter, conversing with the owner or a customer, filled me with a great sadness. How I longed to walk the noisy, crowded streets of Broadway one last time. Odd, the thoughts of a condemned man.

Approximately five minutes later, by the light of a bright moon, I saw a small cabin appear amidst some trees. When we reached the structure (which had boarded up windows with a few bullet holes in them) the old man told us to stop.

"All right, boys," said the old man, as we turned to look at him, "I want you both to walk inside and each of you to sit down on one of my chairs. And, once again, if you got any ideas of trying to get away from me, give them up now. If a man can't shoot two intruders in his own cabin, ain't no place on this here earth that he *can* do any shootin'. Now, get inside. Get!"

The Reb went in first and then I followed behind him. Inside the cabin we found hardback chairs and each sat down on one. In one corner was a stone fireplace where crackling flames cast a pale yellow glow throughout the room. An oil lamp flickered on a table. The walls were unadorned except for one shelf which held a few books. In the dim light I could not read the titles. Across the room was a door which might have led to another room or a closet. In another corner was a coat rack.

"Move them chairs close together," said the old man. "I want them right next to each other."

We did as we were told.

The old man sat down on a chair opposite us and held the gun pointed in our direction. "How rude of me," he said. "I don't know your names. Mine's Samuel."

The Reb sat up stiffly and said, "I am Private—"

"Stop!" said the man. "Ain't no ranks in my home. I just want your Christian name."

"Owen," said the Reb, reluctantly.

"And you?" he said, looking at me.

"It's Andrew," I said.

"Just like the Vice-president," he said.

"He ain't no Vice-president of mine," said Owen, with disdain.

"Oh no?" said Samuel. "And why is that?"

"Come on, man. You live not twenty-five miles from Richmond and have to ask that question? Are you a traitor? Or just a northern spy?"

I had to admit he had a valid question, one I had thought of myself.

"I am neither a traitor nor a spy. I am neutral," said the old man.

"Ain't no one neutral in this war," said Owen. "You are either Union or Confederate and that's a fact."

"You seem to know a lot, boy, how old are you?" said Samuel.

"I'm nineteen," he said, holding up his chin.

"Yup," said Samuel, smirking, "nineteen's about the age when one knows everything."

Now it was my turn to speak. "Sir, I mean you no disrespect, but what do you intend to do with us? Did you bring us to your home simply to have a discussion?"

"You ain't any more polite than your brother, here," said Samuel.

"He ain't no brother of mine," said Owen.

"All men are brothers," said Samuel. "Where you from, Andrew?"

"New York," I said, "born and bred."

"Dirty Yankee," said Owen.

"I'll thank you not to speak unless spoken to, Owen," said Samuel, tilting his gun at the Rebel. "Now then, would anyone like a drink of water?"

My mouth was parched and so apparently was Owen's. After Samuel gave each of us some water from a tin cup he sat back down on the chair in front of us and, still holding the revolver, looked us over. I tried to figure out what he would do next. Would he kill me first or Owen? And why bring us to the cabin at all? Why not simply do the deed outside amidst the lost souls I had encountered only moments earlier? Unless he first meant to see if we possessed any knowledge of our superior's plans.

I put aside speculating upon my captor's motives long enough to think about my sweet Bessie. How I longed to see her beautiful brown eyes, her long chestnut hair and feel the touch of her hand again. Why had I delayed in asking for her father's blessing, and postponed my proposal of marriage? The idea that I had wanted to wait till I became a journeyman in order to receive a higher salary seemed so unimportant now.

"Owen, you never told us where you were from," said Samuel.

"I'm from Georgia," he said, "Two day's ride from Atlanta. Or what's left of it after that devil, Sherman, got finished turning it to rubble." Owen looked at me and sneered.

"I suppose Sherman had a hand in Harper's Ferry, Chickamunga, Cold Harbor, First and Second Manassas and Fredricksburg," I said.

"You can't compare the total destruction of entire cities and thousands of people to—" said Owen.

"That's enough, children," said Samuel, "there's been atrocities on both sides. But that's what war is about, ain't it? Killing as many people as possible?"

"While you sit in your little house out in the forest?" I said.

Samuel squinted at me. "I'll have you know, young man, that I wasn't always a hermit. I was a telegraph operator and a fine one too, till your army cut my wires."

"I knew it!" said Owen, smiling. "You *are* one of us. Now go on, put the Yankee out of his misery," said Owen.

"Shut up," said Samuel. "I'll do the killing when I please and to whom I please."

This quieted down the Reb, who swallowed and slumped in his chair.

"There's been too much bloodshed," said Samuel, softly. "How many thousands of wives are there without husbands? How many children without fathers? It's gone on long enough. Year after bloody year. This here is a great nation. If the war continues we'll all perish, like that fella in Greece, Pyrrhus. His victory cost him everything. When enough people die there ain't no winners anymore. Everyone loses."

"That's a right nice speech," said Owen. "How about I take you to meet General Lee and you can recite it to him personally?"

At this, I watched Samuel slowly stand up. Uh-oh, I thought, now the Reb's gone and done it. He's opened his mouth once too often and he's going to get us killed for sure.

Samuel moved away from his chair and took a few steps back while still keeping the gun trained on us. Then he said, "Stand up, both of you."

I stood up as did Owen. Here it comes, I thought. I closed my eyes and said a silent prayer. The old man would undoubtedly shoot us then toss our bodies outside. Wild animals would no doubt devour our remains.

"Strip off your uniforms," said Samuel.

I glanced at Owen and he at me. Was I in some strange morphine dream?

"You heard me," said Samuel. "Take off your uniforms. You can keep on your undergarments."

Neither Owen nor I moved. Samuel held his gun and took a step closer. I began undoing the nine brass eagle buttons on my frock coat.

"Your brogans too," said Samuel, pointing at my feet.

I removed my boots. In a few seconds I had my uniform and kepi in my hands.

"Throw them all in a heap on the floor," said Samuel.

My dark blue coat, cap, trousers and boots landed first and then Owen's gray ones fell on top of mine. Samuel went over to the uniforms, picked them up, and, with one motion tossed the pile of clothing into the fireplace. The flames immediately began their work and shortly all that remained were ashes.

"All right, boys," said Samuel, reaching for some rope on a nearby table, "sit down on your chairs."

"I don't reckon I understand any of this," said Owen. "What's the idea of burning our clothes?"

"Just be glad it's your clothes I'm burning and not you," said Samuel. "Now, sit down."

We did, as Samuel placed the gun in his left hand, pulled out an Arms D Guard Bowie knife and cut a piece of rope. He threw the rope piece to Owen and said, "Tie Andrew to his chair."

Owen picked up the rope and lashed my wrists to the back of my chair with great vigor. After fashioning what felt like elaborate knots, he tested them a couple of times, then, apparently satisfied with their strength, turned to Samuel.

"Now what would you like me to do?" said Owen. "I could interrogate him regarding troop movements—"

"Sit down on your chair and place your hands behind your back," said Samuel, as he came over with the rope. He cut off a piece and tied Owen's hands to the back of the chair. When he was done he stood up.

"I am puzzled," I said. "First you preach peace then you have us disrobe and bind us to chairs. You seem as warring as the armies you claim to have contempt for."

"A good observation, however, the difference is, thus far I have only threatened violence while *your* armies are doing far more than that."

"I don't understand," said Owen. "Here you are, living practically within spitting distance of the capital of the Confederacy, and yet you profess to hate both sides. Why?"

I saw Samuel stare at us and then, for the first time since we'd entered the cabin, he looked away, toward one of the boarded up windows. For a minute or two he said nothing. Then he turned and faced us again.

"I supposed it don't hurt none to tell you. My wife was killed by a Union army man. We'd just celebrated our thirty-fifth wedding anniversary."

"A Union man," said Owen, nodding his head and looking at me with a kind of sardonic smile.

"I'd been out of town trying to get some new relays for my switchboard, my telegraph, and when I got back half the town lay in ruins. And my beloved, Violet…" I saw him blink a few times and wipe his eyes with his sleeve.

"Untie me," said Owen. "You hate the Yankees as much as I do."

"I ain't done yet," he said. "I neglected to mention my son, Clayton. He was about your age when he joined up. They sent him to some godforsaken battlefield. All I know is, he come back in a box. Turned out he was shot by someone in his own regiment. I been told it ain't that uncommon an occurrence. Apparently the smoke from the gunpowder and cannon fire can turn the landscape into a cloudy white sheet. A man can't see his own hand in front of his face."

"It was an accident?" asked Owen.

"Of course it was an accident but that don't make him any less dead. That's right, boys, you see, I've had enough of this damn war, of all wars forever. Now, I'm going to go to my bedroom over there and get some sleep. I suggest you try to have yourself a little rest as well."

Samuel went to the front door, locked it, pocketed the key, then walked into the bedroom and closed the door.

I looked back at Owen. He gave me a mean stare.

"We should try to get out of here," I said. "Tomorrow he'll more than likely shoot us. Probably wants to execute us at dawn."

"What do you mean, 'we,' Billy Yank?"

"Listen," I said, "this man is insane, you heard him. His gun doesn't care which of us is blue or which is gray. We've got to work together here."

"Together?" he said, as if he'd just drank some lemon juice.

"That's right, because if we don't help each other we'll both be dead. And it'll be for nothing. It won't be for the glory of the North *or* the South. What are you going to do when you get to heaven and they ask you how you died? Tell them it was on the field of battle as a hero, fighting for what you believed in or on the filthy floor of some crazy old man's cabin for no good reason at all. Think about it, Owen."

It was the first time I had said his name out loud. It felt unnatural, the way it does when you learn a word of a foreign language and then try to pronounce it. I saw Owen look at the ceiling.

After some time he turned back in my direction. "What'd you have in mind?" he said.

"The first thing we need to do is get out of these ropes. Let's move our chairs back to back and each try to undo the other's bonds."

He nodded and we shifted our chairs around. I felt his fingers on my ropes and then I moved mine upon his. For a few moments we worked in silence. I listened to the sound of our breathing and thought about how hungry I was.

"I sure would fancy some pepperpot about now," I said.

"What's that?" said Owen.

"It's a wonderful tasting stew made of tripe and doughballs. My mouth waters at the thought."

"I can't say as I'd turn down some sweet potato pie myself."

"My girl, Bessie, makes the best pepperpot in the world."

"Well, my gal, Louisa, can bake a cracklin' bread that just about melts in your mouth, why the very smell of it alone is enough to send you…" Owen's voice trailed off.

I felt his fingers start to loosen the knots of my rope. Even so, the added pressure made the rope burn into my wrists.

"What did you do before you were conscripted?" I said, pulling on his rope.

"I volunteered, but before that I was a farmer. My family owns a small farm. We grow the best corn in two counties, ask anyone. How about yourself?"

"I'm a printer, actually still an apprentice."

I managed to loosen Owen's rope a little. "Now, just so you don't get all kinds of thoughts," I said, "if you get out of your ropes first and decide to leave me and try to break down that front door, the old man will hear you and shoot you for sure. But if we are together I can help disarm him and we can get the key to the door."

"Now you're my helper, Billy Yank?"

"Just for the duration of our imprisonment in this cabin, Johnny Reb."

"Have it your way," said Owen, as I felt him loosening my rope.

As it happened, I was out of mine first. I got up and continued working on his. Eventually, his rope slipped to the floor.

Owen went over to the table and picked up the oil lamp while I got a small log from next to the fireplace to use as a weapon.

"C'mon," I said, as we quietly made our way toward the bedroom door. When we got there, I put my ear to it and heard snoring. "It sounds like he's asleep," I said, silently testing the doorknob. It was unlocked.

We opened the door and went inside the room. The old man woke up and reached for the gun which was on his night table, but I got to it first. I dropped the piece of firewood and held the revolver steady.

"So," said Samuel, "this is the way it's going to be, is it?" From under his pillow he grabbed his knife and lunged toward us.

I fired the gun and he dropped to the floor.

"You got me," he said, smiling. "I guess my plan worked."

"How's that, old man?" said Owen.

"I wanted you boys to murder me," he said, touching his bloody chest. "I didn't want to live no more. It ain't no life being alone, ain't no life living with this war."

"Why all the political debating?" I asked.

"And why'd you make us take off our uniforms?" said Owen.

"To show you that you're both the same, just boys. Men now. I figured I'd tie you up and then you'd have to put your differences aside against a common enemy. Me. If a couple of young bucks like you can do it maybe the world's got a chance yet."

"There might be a doctor we could take you to," I said.

"Forget it," he replied. "Besides, I want to die. You two were the answer to months of prayers."

Samuel lay real still and his eyes stared straight ahead, unblinking. I closed his lids. Owen reached into Samuel's pocket and took out his key.

We went into the other room. I took a couple of deep breaths and set the gun down on the table.

"He was a peculiar old man," said Owen.

"Yes," I said, as I noticed the coat rack in one corner of the room. I went over, took a brown colored coat off a hook and tossed it to Owen. "Here," I said, "no point in running around in our undergarments."

I put on another coat, this one black, and headed toward him. To my surprise, Owen now had the gun in his hand and was pointing it at my heart. "Are you going to shoot me?" I asked.

He stared into my eyes for a long time, then replied, "I don't shoot civilians."

After that, he unlocked the door, stepped outside and disappeared into the night.

I lingered by the open door looking at the shadowy trees. A moment later I walked out of the cabin toward the quiet darkness beyond.

✗

"DON'T DO WHAT WE TELL YOU TO DO BECAUSE WE'RE YOUR PARENTS. DO WHAT WE TELL YOU TO DO BECAUSE WE'RE BOTH ATTORNEYS AND WON'T HESITATE TO SUE YOU."

A SCANDAL IN BOHEMIA

by Arthur Conan Doyle

I

To Sherlock Holmes she is always *the* woman. I have seldom heard him mention her under any other name. In h©dis eyes she eclipses and predominates the whole of her sex. It was not that he felt any emotion akin to love for Irene Adler. All emotions, and that one particularly, were abhorrent to his cold, precise but admirably balanced mind. He was, I take it, the most perfect reasoning and observing machine that the world has seen, but as a lover he would have placed himself in a false position. He never spoke of the softer passions, save with a gibe and a sneer. They were admirable things for the observer — excellent for drawing the veil from men's motives and actions. But for the trained reasoner to admit such intrusions into his own delicate and finely adjusted temperament was to introduce a distracting factor which might throw a doubt upon all his mental results. Grit in a ©sensitive instrument, or a crack in one of his own high-power lenses, would not be more disturbing than a strong emotion in a nature such as his. And yet there was but one woman to him, and that woman was the late Irene Adler, of dubious and questionable memory.

I had seen little of Holmes lately. My marriage had drifted us away from each other. My own complete happiness, and the home-centred interests which rise up around the man who first finds himself master of his own establishment, were sufficient to absorb all my attention, while Holmes, who loathed every form of society with his whole Bohemian soul, remained in our lodgings in Baker Street, buried among his old books, and alternating from week to week between cocaine and ambition, the drowsiness of the drug, and the fierce energy of his own keen nature. He was still, as ever, deeply attracted by the study of crime, and occupied his immense faculties and extraordinary powers of observation in following out those clues, and clearing up those mysteries which had been abandoned as hopeless by the official police. From time to time I heard some vague account of his doings: of his summons to Odessa in the case of the Trepoff murder, of his clearing up of the singular tragedy of the Atkinson brothers at Trincomalee, and finally of the mission which he had accomplished so delicately and successfully for the reigning family of Holland. Beyond these signs of his activity, however, which I merely shared with all the readers of the daily press, I knew little of my former friend and companion.

One night — it was on the twentieth of March, 1888 — I was returning from a journey to a patient (for I had now returned to civil practice), when my way led me through Baker Street. As I passed the well-remembered door, which must always be associated in my mind with my wooing, and with the dark incidents of the Study in Scarlet, I was seized with a keen desire to see Holmes again, and to know how he was employing his extraordinary powers. His rooms were brilliantly lit, and, even as I looked up, I saw his tall, spare figure pass twice in a dark silhouette against the blind. He was pacing the room swiftly, eagerly, with his head sunk upon his chest and his hands clasped behind him. To me, who knew his every mood and habit, his attitude and manner told their own story. He was at work again. He had risen out of his drug-created dreams and was hot upon the scent of some new problem. I rang the bell and was shown up to the chamber which had formerly been in part my own.

His manner was not effusive. It seldom was; but he was glad, I think, to see me. With hardly a word spoken, but with a kindly eye, he waved me to an armchair, threw across his case of cigars, and indicated a spirit case and a gasogene in the corner. Then he stood before the fire and looked me over in his singular introspective fashion.

"Wedlock suits you," he remarked. I think, Watson, that you have put on seven and a half pounds since I saw you."

"Seven!" I answered.

Indeed, I should have thought a little more. Just a trifle more, I fancy, Watson. And in practice again, I observe. You did not tell me that you intended to go into harness."

"Then, how do you know?"

I see it, I deduce it. How do I know that you have been getting yourself very wet lately, and that you have a most clumsy and careless servant girl?"

"My dear Holmes," said I, this is too much. You would certainly have been burned, had you lived a few centuries ago. It is true that I had a country walk on Thursday and came home in a dreadful mess, but as I have changed my clothes I can't imagine how you deduce it. As to Mary Jane, she is incorrigible, and my wife has given her notice, but there, again, I fail to see how you work it out."

He chuckled to himself and rubbed his long, nervous hands together.

"It is simplicity itself," said he; my eyes tell me that on the inside of your left shoe, just where the firelight strikes it, the leather is scored by six almost parallel cuts. Obviously they have been caused by someone who has very carelessly scraped round the edges of the sole in order to remove crusted mud from it. Hence, you see, my double deduction that you had been out in vile weather, and that you had a particularly malignant boot-slitting specimen of the London slavey. As to your practice, if a gentleman walks into my rooms smelling of iodoform, with a black mark of nitrate of silver upon his right forefinger, and a bulge on the right side of his top-hat to show where he has secreted his stethoscope, I must be dull, indeed, if I do not pronounce him to be an active member of the medical profession."

I could not help laughing at the ease with which he explained his process of deduction. "When I hear you give your reasons," I remarked, "the thing always appears to me to be so ridiculously simple that I could easily do it myself, though at each successive instance of your reasoning I am baffled until you explain your process. And yet I believe that my eyes are as good as yours."

"Quite so," he answered, lighting a cigarette, and throwing himself down into an armchair. "You see, but you do not observe. The distinction is clear. For example, you have frequently seen the steps which lead up from the hall to this room."

"Frequently."

How often?

"Well, some hundreds of times."

Then how many are there?"

"How many? I don't know."

"Quite so! You have not observed. And yet you have seen. That is just my point. Now, I know that there are seventeen steps, because I have both seen and observed. By the way, since you are interested in these little problems, and since you are good enough to chronicle one or two of my trifling experiences, you may be interested in this." He threw over a sheet of thick, pink-tinted note-paper which had been lying open upon the table. "It came by the last post," said he. "Read it aloud."

The note was undated, and without either signature or address.

> There will call upon you to-night, at a quarter to eight o'clock [it said], a gentleman who desires to consult you upon a matter of the very deepest moment. Your recent services to one of the royal houses of Europe have shown that you are one who may safely be trusted with matters which are of an importance which can hardly be exaggerated. This account of you we have from all quarters received. Be in your chamber then at that hour, and do not take it amiss if your visitor wear a mask.

"This is indeed a mystery," I remarked. "What do you imagine that it means?"

"I have no data yet. It is a capital mistake to theorize before one has data. Insensibly one begins to twist facts to suit theories, instead of theories to suit facts. But the note itself. What do you deduce from it?"

I carefully examined the writing, and the paper upon which it was written.

"The man who wrote it was presumably well to do," I remarked, endeavouring to imitate my companion's processes. "Such paper could not be bought under half a crown a packet. It is peculiarly strong and stiff."

"Peculiar — that is the very word," said Holmes. "It is not an English paper at all. Hold it up to the light."

I did so, and saw a large "E" with a small g, a "P," and a large G with a small "f" woven into the texture of the paper.

"What do you make of that?" asked Holmes.

"The name of the maker, no doubt; or his monogram, rather."

"Not at all. The "G" with the small "t" stands for 'Gesellschaft,' which is the German for "Company." It is a customary contraction like our "Co." `P,' of course, stands for "Papier." Now for the `Eg.' Let us glance at our Continental Gazetteer." He took down a heavy brown volume from his shelves. "Eglow, Eglonitz — here we are, Egria. It is in a German-speaking country — in Bohemia, not far from Carlsbad. "Remarkable as being the scene of the death of Wallenstein, and for its numerous glass-factories and paper-mills." Ha, ha, my boy, what do you make of that?" His eyes sparkled, and he sent up a great blue triumphant cloud from his cigarette.

"The paper was made in Bohemia," I said.

"Precisely. And the man who wrote the note is a German. Do you note the peculiar construction of the sentence — "This account of you we have from all quarters received." A Frenchman or Russian could not have written that. It is the German who is so uncourteous to his verbs. It only remains, therefore, to discover what is wanted by this German who writes upon Bohemian paper and prefers wearing a mask to showing his face. And here he comes, if I am not mistaken, to resolve all our doubts."

As he spoke there was the sharp sound of horses' hoofs and grating wheels against the curb, followed by a sharp pull at the bell. Holmes whistled.

"A pair, by the sound," said he. Yes, he continued, glancing out of the window. "A nice little brougham and a pair of beauties. A hundred and fifty guineas apiece. There's money in this case, Watson, if there is nothing else."

"I think that I had better go, Holmes."

"Not a bit, Doctor. Stay where you are. I am lost without my Boswell. And this promises to be interesting. It would be a pity to miss it."

"But your client — "

Never mind him. I may want your help, and so may he. Here he comes. Sit down in that armchair, Doctor, and give us your best attention."

A slow and heavy step, which had been heard upon the stairs and in the passage, paused immediately outside the door. Then there was a loud and authoritative tap.

"Come in!" said Holmes.

A man entered who could hardly have been less than six feet six inches in height, with the chest and limbs of a Hercules. His dress was rich with a richness which would, in England, be looked upon as akin to bad taste. Heavy bands of astrakhan were slashed across the sleeves and fronts of his double-breasted coat, while the deep blue cloak which was thrown over his shoulders was lined with flame-coloured silk and secured at the neck with a brooch which consisted of a single flaming beryl. Boots which extended halfway up his calves, and which were trimmed at the tops with rich brown fur, completed the impression of barbaric opulence which was suggested by his whole appearance. He carried a broad-brimmed hat in his hand, while he wore across the upper part of his face, extending down past the cheekbones, a black vizard mask, which he had apparently adjusted that very moment, for his hand was still raised to it as he entered. From the lower part of the face he appeared to be a man of strong character, with a thick, hanging lip, and a long, straight chin suggestive of resolution pushed to the length of obstinacy.

"You had my note?" he asked with a deep harsh voice and a strongly marked German accent. "I told you that I would call." He looked from one to the other of us, as if uncertain which to address.

"Pray take a seat," said Holmes. This is my friend and colleague, Dr. Watson, who is occasionally good enough to help me in my cases. Whom have I the honour to address?"

"You may address me as the Count Von Kramm, a Bohemian nobleman. I understand that this gentleman, your friend, is a man of honour and discretion, whom I may trust with a matter of the most extreme importance. If not, I should much prefer to communicate with you alone."

I rose to go, but Holmes caught me by the wrist and pushed me back into my chair. "It is both, or none," said he. "You may say before this gentleman anything which you may say to me."

The Count shrugged his broad shoulders. "Then I must begin," said he, "by binding you both to absolute secrecy for two years; at the end of that time the matter will be of no importance. At present it is not too much to say that it is of such weight it may have an influence upon European history."

"I promise," said Holmes.

"And I."

"You will excuse this mask," continued our strange visitor. "The august person who employs me wishes his agent to be unknown to you, and I may confess at once that the title by which I have just called myself is not exactly my own."

"I was aware of it," said Holmes drily.

"The circumstances are of great delicacy, and every precaution has to be taken to quench what might grow to be an immense scandal and seriously compromise one of the reigning families of Europe. To speak plainly, the matter implicates the great House of Ormstein, hereditary kings of Bohemia."

"I was also aware of that," murmured Holmes, settling himself down in his armchair and closing his eyes.

Our visitor glanced with some apparent surprise at the languid, lounging figure of the man who had been no doubt depicted to him as the most incisive reasoner and most energetic agent in Europe. Holmes slowly reopened his eyes and looked impatiently at his gigantic client.

"If your Majesty would condescend to state your case," he remarked, "I should be better able to advise you."

The man sprang from his chair and paced up and down the room in uncontrollable agitation. Then, with a gesture of desperation, he tore the mask from his face and hurled it upon the ground.

"You are right," he cried; I am the King. Why should I attempt to conceal it?"

"Why, indeed?" murmured Holmes. Your Majesty had not spoken before I was aware that I was addressing Wilhelm Gottsreich Sigismond von Ormstein, Grand Duke of Cassel-Felstein, and hereditary King of Bohemia."

"But you can understand," said our strange visitor, sitting down once more and passing his hand over his high white forehead, "you can understand that I am not accustomed to doing such business in my own person. Yet the matter was so delicate that I could not confide it to an agent without putting myself in his power. I have come incognito from Prague for the purpose of consulting you."

"Then, pray consult," said Holmes, shutting his eyes once more.

"The facts are briefly these: Some five years ago, during a lengthy visit to Warsaw, I made the acquaintance of the wellknown adventuress, Irene Adler. The name is no doubt familiar to you."

"Kindly look her up in my index, Doctor," murmured Holmes without opening his eyes. For many years he had adopted a system of docketing all paragraphs concerning men and things, so that it was difficult to name a subject or a person on which he could not at once furnish information. In this case I found her biography sandwiched in between that of a Hebrew rabbi and that of a staff-commander who had written a monograph upon the deep-sea fishes.

"Let me see!" said Holmes. Hum! Born in New Jersey in the year 1858. Contralto — hum! La Scala, hum! Prima donna Imperial Opera of Warsaw — yes! Retired from operatic stage — ha! Living in London — quite so! Your Majesty, as I understand, became entangled with this young person, wrote her some compromising letters, and is now desirous of getting those letters back."

"Precisely so. But how — "

"Was there a secret marriage?"

"None."

No legal papers or certificates?"

"None."

Then I fail to follow your Majesty. If this young person should produce her letters for blackmailing or other purposes, how is she to prove their authenticity?"

"There is the writing."

Pooh, pooh! Forgery."

"My private note-paper."

"Stolen."

"My own seal."

Imitated.

"My photograph."

Bought.

"We were both in the photograph."

"Oh, dear! That is very bad! Your Majesty has indeed committed an indiscretion."

"I was mad — insane."

You have compromised yourself seriously."

"I was only Crown Prince then. I was young. I am but thirty now."

"It must be recovered."

We have tried and failed."

"Your Majesty must pay. It must be bought."

"She will not sell."

"Stolen, then."

Five attempts have been made. Twice burglars in my pay ransacked her house. Once we diverted her luggage when she travelled. Twice she has been waylaid. There has been no result."

"No sign of it?"

Absolutely none."

Holmes laughed. "It is quite a pretty little problem," said he.

"But a very serious one to me," returned the King reproachfully.

"Very, indeed. And what does she propose to do with the photograph?"

"To ruin me."

But how?

"I am about to be married."

So I have heard."

"To Clotilde Lothman von Saxe-Meningen, second daughter of the King of Scandinavia. You may know the strict principles of her family. She is herself the very soul of delicacy. A shadow of a doubt as to my conduct would bring the matter to an end."

"And Irene Adler?"

Threatens to send them the photograph. And she will do it. I know that she will do it. You do not know her, but she has a soul of steel. She has the face of the most beautiful of women, and the mind of the most resolute of men. Rather than I should marry another woman, there are no lengths to which she would not go — none."

"You are sure that she has not sent it yet?"

"I am sure."

"And why?"

Because she has said that she would send it on the day when the betrothal was publicly proclaimed. That will be next Monday."

"Oh, then we have three days yet," said Holmes with a yawn. "That is very fortunate, as I have one or two matters of importance to look into just at present. Your Majesty will, of course, stay in London for the present?"

"Certainly. You will find me at the Langham under the name of the Count Von Kramm."

"Then I shall drop you a line to let you know how we progress."

"Pray do so. I shall be all anxiety."

"Then, as to money?"

"You have carte blanche."

"Absolutely?"

"I tell you that I would give one of the provinces of my kingdom to have that photograph."

"And for present expenses?"

The King took a heavy chamois leather bag from under his cloak and laid it on the table.

"There are three hundred pounds in gold and seven hundred in notes," he said.

Holmes scribbled a receipt upon a sheet of his note-book and handed it to him.

"And Mademoiselle's address?" he asked.

"Is Briony Lodge, Serpentine Avenue, St. John's Wood."

Holmes took a note of it. "One other question," said he. "Was the photograph a cabinet?"

"It was."

Then, good-night, your Majesty, and I trust that we shall soon have some good news for you. And good-night, Watson," he added, as the wheels of the royal brougham rolled down the street. "If you will be good enough to call to-morrow afternoon at three o'clock I should like to chat this little matter over with you."

II

At three o'clock precisely I was at Baker Street, but Holmes had not yet returned. The landlady informed me that he had left the house shortly after eight o'clock in the morning. I sat down beside the fire, however, with the intention of awaiting him, however long he might be. I was already deeply interested in his inquiry, for, though it was surrounded by none of the grim and strange features which were associated with the two crimes which I have already recorded, still, the nature of the case and the exalted station of his client gave it a character of its own. Indeed, apart from the nature of the investigation which my friend had on hand, there was something in his masterly grasp of a situation, and his keen, incisive reasoning, which made it a pleasure to me to study his system of work, and to follow the quick, subtle methods by which he disentangled the most inextricable mysteries. So accustomed was I to his invariable success that the very possibility of his failing had ceased to enter into my head.

It was close upon four before the door opened, and a drunken-looking groom, ill-kempt and side-whiskered, with an inflamed face and disreputable clothes, walked into the room.

Accustomed as I was to my friend's amazing powers in the use of disguises, I had to look three times before I was certain that it was indeed he. With a nod he vanished into the bedroom, whence he emerged in five minutes tweed-suited and respectable, as of old. Putting his hands into his pockets, he stretched out his legs in front of the fire and laughed heartily for some minutes.

"Well, really!" he cried, and then he choked and laughed again until he was obliged to lie back, limp and helpless, in the chair.

"What is it?"

"It's quite too funny. I am sure you could never guess how I employed my morning, or what I ended by doing."

"I can't imagine. I suppose that you have been watching the habits, and perhaps the house, of Miss Irene Adler."

"Quite so; but the sequel was rather unusual. I will tell you, however. I left the house a little after eight o'clock this morning in the character of a groom out of work. There is a wonderful sympathy and freemasonry among horsy men. Be one of them, and you will know all that there is to know. I soon found Briony Lodge. It is a bijou villa, with a garden at the back, but built out in front right up to the road, two stories. Chubb lock to the door. Large sitting-room on the right side, well furnished, with long windows almost to the floor, and those preposterous English window fasteners which a child could open. Behind there was nothing remarkable, save that the passage window could be reached from the top of the coach-house. I walked round it and examined it closely from every point of view, but without noting anything else of interest.

"I then lounged down the street and found, as I expected, that there was a mews in a lane which runs down by one wall of the garden. I lent the ostlers a hand in rubbing down their horses, and received in exchange twopence, a glass of half and half, two fills of shag tobacco, and as much information as I could desire about Miss Adler, to say nothing of half a dozen other people in the neighbourhood in whom I was not in the least interested, but whose biographies I was compelled to listen to."

"And what of Irene Adler?" I asked.

"Oh, she has turned all the men's heads down in that part. She is the daintiest thing under a bonnet on this planet. So say the Serpentine-mews, to a man. She lives quietly, sings at concerts, drives out at five every day, and returns at seven sharp for dinner. Seldom goes out at other times, except when she sings. Has only one male visitor, but a good deal of him. He is dark, handsome, and dashing, never calls less than once a day, and often twice. He is a Mr Godfrey Norton, of the Inner Temple. See the advantages of a cabman as a confidant. They had driven him home a dozen times from Serpentine-mews, and knew all about him. When I had listened to all they had to tell, I began to walk up and down near Briony Lodge once more, and to think over my plan of campaign.

"This Godfrey Norton was evidently an important factor in the matter. He was a lawyer. That sounded ominous. What was the relation between them, and what the object of his repeated visits? Was she his client, his friend, or his mistress? If the former, she had probably transferred the photograph to his keeping. If the latter, it was less likely. On the issue of this question depended whether I should continue my work at Briony Lodge, or turn my attention to the gentleman's chambers in the Temple. It was a delicate point, and it widened the field of my inquiry. I fear that I bore you with these details, but I have to let you see my little difficulties, if you are to understand the situation."

"I am following you closely," I answered.

"I was still balancing the matter in my mind when a hansom cab drove up to Briony Lodge, and a gentleman sprang out. He was a remarkably handsome man, dark, aquiline, and moustached — evidently the man of whom I had heard. He appeared to be in a great hurry, shouted to the cabman to wait, and brushed past the maid who opened the door with the air of a man who was thoroughly at home.

"He was in the house about half an hour, and I could catch glimpses of him in the windows of the sitting-room, pacing up and down, talking excitedly, and waving his arms. Of her I could see nothing. Presently he emerged, looking even more flurried than before. As he stepped up to the cab, he pulled a gold watch from his pocket and looked at it earnestly, 'Drive like the devil,' he shouted, 'first to Gross & Hankey's in Regent Street, and then to the Church of St. Monica in the Edgeware Road. Half a guinea if you do it in twenty minutes!'

"Away they went, and I was just wondering whether I should not do well to follow them when up the lane came a neat little landau, the coachman with his coat only half-buttoned, and his tie under his ear, while all the tags of his harness were sticking out of the buckles. It hadn't pulled up before she shot out of the hall door and into it. I only caught a glimpse of her at the moment, but she was a lovely woman, with a face that a man might die for.

"'The Church of St. Monica, John,' she cried, 'and half a sovereign if you reach it in twenty minutes.'

"This was quite too good to lose, Watson. I was just balancing whether I should run for it, or whether I should perch behind her landau when a cab came through the street. The driver looked twice at such a shabby fare, but I jumped in before he could object. 'The Church of St. Monica,' said I, 'and half a sovereign if you reach it in twenty minutes.' It was twenty-five minutes to twelve, and of course it was clear enough what was in the wind.

"My cabby drove fast. I don't think I ever drove faster, but the others were there before us. The cab and the landau with their steaming horses were in front of the door when I arrived. I paid the man and hurried into the church. There was not a soul there save the two whom I had followed and a surpliced clergyman, who seemed to be expostulating with them. They were all three standing in a knot in front of the altar. I lounged up the side aisle like any other idler who has dropped into a church. Suddenly, to my surprise, the three at the altar faced round to me, and Godfrey Norton came running as hard as he could towards me.

"'Thank God,' he cried. 'You'll do. Come! Come!'

"'What then?' I asked.

"'Come, man, come, only three minutes, or it won't be legal.'

"I was half-dragged up to the altar, and before I knew where I was I found myself mumbling responses which were whispered in my ear, and vouching for things of which I knew nothing, and generally assisting in the secure tying up of Irene Adler, spinster, to Godfrey Norton, bachelor. It was all done in an instant, and there was the gentleman thanking me on the one side and the lady on the other, while the clergyman beamed on me in front. It was the most preposterous position in which I ever found myself in my life, and it was the thought of it that started me laughing just now. It seems that there had been some informality about their license, that the clergyman absolutely refused to marry them without a witness of some sort, and that my lucky appearance saved the bridegroom from having to sally out into the streets in search of a best man. The bride gave me a sovereign, and I mean to wear it on my watch-chain in memory of the occasion.

"This is a very unexpected turn of affairs," said I; "and what then?"

"Well, I found my plans very seriously menaced. It looked as if the pair might take an immediate departure, and so necessitate very prompt and energetic measures on my part. At the church door, however, they separated, he driving back to the Temple, and she to her own house. 'I shall drive out in the park at five as usual,'she said as she left him. I heard no more. They drove away in different directions, and I went off to make my own arrangements."

"Which are?"

"Some cold beef and a glass of beer," he answered, ringing the bell. "I have been too busy to think of food, and I am likely to be busier still this evening. By the way, Doctor, I shall want your cooperation."

"I shall be delighted."

"You don't mind breaking the law?"

"Not in the least."

"Nor running a chance of arrest?"

"Not in a good cause."

"Oh, the cause is excellent!"

"Then I am your man."

"I was sure that I might rely on you."

"But what is it you wish?"

"When Mrs Turner has brought in the tray I will make it clear to you. Now," he said as he turned hungrily on the simple fare that our landlady had provided, "I must discuss it while I eat, for I have not much time. It is nearly five now. In two hours we must be on the scene of action. Miss Irene, or Madame, rather, returns from her drive at seven. We must be at Briony Lodge to meet her."

"And what then?"

"You must leave that to me. I have already arranged what is to occur. There is only one point on which I must insist. You must not interfere, come what may. You understand?"

"I am to be neutral?"

"To do nothing whatever. There will probably be some small unpleasantness. Do not join in it. It will end in my being conveyed into the house. Four or five minutes afterwards the sitting-room window will open. You are to station yourself close to that open window."

"Yes."

"You are to watch me, for I will be visible to you."

"Yes."

"And when I raise my hand — so — you will throw into the room what I give you to throw, and will, at the same time, raise the cry of fire. You quite follow me?"

"Entirely."

"It is nothing very formidable," he said, taking a long cigar-shaped roll from his pocket. "It is an ordinary plumber's smoke-rocket, fitted with a cap at either end to make it self-lighting. Your task is confined to that. When you raise your cry of fire, it will be taken up by quite a number of people. You may then walk to the end of the street, and I will rejoin you in ten minutes. I hope that I have made myself clear?"

"I am to remain neutral, to get near the window, to watch you, and at the signal to throw in this object, then to raise the cry of fire, and to wait you at the comer of the street."

"Precisely."

"Then you may entirely rely on me."

"That is excellent. I think, perhaps, it is almost time that I prepare for the new role I have to play."

He disappeared into his bedroom and returned in a few minutes in the character of an amiable and simple-minded Nonconformist clergyman. His broad black hat, his baggy trousers, his white tie, his sympathetic smile, and general look of peering and benevolent curiosity were such as Mr John Hare alone could have equalled. It was not merely that Holmes changed his costume. His expression, his manner, his very soul seemed to vary with every fresh part that he assumed. The stage lost a fine actor, even as science lost an acute reasoner, when he became a specialist in crime.

It was a quarter past six when we left Baker Street, and it still wanted ten minutes to the hour when we found ourselves in Serpentine Avenue. It was already dusk, and the lamps were just being lighted as we paced up and down in front of Briony Lodge, waiting for the coming of its occupant. The house was just such as I had pictured it from Sherlock Holmes's succinct description, but the locality appeared to be less private than I expected. On the contrary, for a small street in a quiet neighbourhood, it was remarkably animated. There was a group of shabbily dressed men smoking and laughing in a corner, a scissors-grinder with his wheel, two guardsmen who were flirting with a nurse-girl, and several well-dressed young men who were lounging up and down with cigars in their mouths.

"You see," remarked Holmes, as we paced to and fro in front of the house, "this marriage rather simplifies matters. The photograph becomes a double-edged weapon now. The chances are that she would be as averse to its being seen by Mr Godfrey Norton, as our client is to its coming to the eyes of his princess. Now the question is, Where are we to find the photograph?"

"Where, indeed?"

"It is most unlikely that she carries it about with her. It is cabinet size. Too large for easy concealment about a woman's dress. She knows that the King is capable of having her waylaid and searched. Two attempts of the sort have already been made. We may take it, then, that she does not carry it about with her."

"Where, then?"

"Her banker or her lawyer. There is that double possibility. But I am inclined to think neither. Women are naturally secretive, and they like to do their own secreting. Why should she hand it over to anyone else? She could trust her own guardianship, but she could not tell what indirect or political influence might be brought to bear upon a business man. Besides, remember that she had resolved to use it within a few days. It must be where she can lay her hands upon it. It must be in her own house."

"But it has twice been burgled."

"Pshaw! They did not know how to look."

"But how will you look?"

"I will not look."

"What then?"

"I will get her to show me."

"But she will refuse."

"She will not be able to. But I hear the rumble of wheels. It is her carriage. Now carry out my orders to the letter."

As he spoke the gleam of the side-lights of a carriage came round the curve of the avenue. It was a smart little landau which rattled up to the door of Briony Lodge. As it pulled up, one of the loafing men at the corner dashed forward to open the door in the hope of earning a copper, but was elbowed away by another loafer, who had rushed up with the same intention. A fierce quarrel broke out, which was increased by the two guardsmen, who took sides with one of the loungers, and by the scissors-grinder, who was equally hot upon the other side. A blow was struck, and in an instant the lady, who had stepped from her carriage, was the centre of a little knot of flushed and struggling men, who struck savagely at each other with their fists and sticks. Holmes dashed into the crowd to protect the lady; but just as he reached her he gave a cry and dropped to the ground, with the blood running freely down his face. At his fall the guardsmen took to their heels in one direction and the loungers in the other, while a number of better-dressed people, who had watched the scuffle without taking part in it, crowded in to help the lady and to attend to the injured man. Irene Adler, as I will still call her, had hurried up the steps; but she stood at the top with her superb figure outlined against the lights of the hall, looking back into the street.

"Is the poor gentleman much hurt?" she asked.

"He is dead," cried several voices.

"No, no, there's life in him!" shouted another. "But he'll be gone before you can get him to hospital."

"He's a brave fellow," said a woman. They would have had the lady's purse and watch if it hadn't been for him. They were a gang, and a rough one, too. Ah, he's breathing now."

"He can't lie in the street. May we bring him in, marm?"

"Surely. Bring him into the sitting-room. There is a comfortable sofa. This way, please!"

Slowly and solemnly he was borne into Briony Lodge and laid out in the principal room, while I still observed the proceedings from my post by the window. The lamps had been lit, but the blinds had not been drawn, so that I could see Holmes as he lay upon the couch. I do not know whether he was seized with compunction at that moment for the part he was playing, but I know that I never felt more heartily ashamed of myself in my life than when I saw the beautiful creature against whom I was conspiring, or the grace and kindliness with which she waited upon the injured man. And yet it would be the blackest treachery to Holmes to draw back now from the part which he had intrusted to me. I hardened my heart, and took the smoke-rocket from under my ulster. After all, I thought, we are not injuring her. We are but preventing her from injuring another.

Holmes had sat up upon the couch, and I saw him motion like a man who is in need of air. A maid rushed across and threw open the window. At the same instant I saw him raise his hand and at the signal I tossed my rocket into the room with a cry of "Fire!" The word was no sooner out of my mouth than the whole crowd of spectators, well dressed and ill — gentlemen, ostlers, and servant-maids — joined in a general shriek of "Fire!" Thick clouds of smoke curled through the room and out at the open window. I caught a glimpse of rushing figures, and a moment later the voice of Holmes from within assuring them that it was a false alarm. Slipping through the shouting crowd I made my way to the corner of the street, and in ten minutes was rejoiced to find my friend's arm in mine, and to get away from the scene of uproar. He walked swiftly and in silence for some few minutes until we had turned down one of the quiet streets which lead towards the Edgeware Road.

"You did it very nicely, Doctor," he remarked. "Nothing could have been better. It is all right."

"You have the photograph?"

"I know where it is."

"And how did you find out?"

"She showed me, as I told you she would."

"I am still in the dark."

"I do not wish to make a mystery," said he, laughing. "The matter was perfectly simple. You, of course, saw that everyone in the street was an accomplice. They were all engaged for the evening."

"I guessed as much."

"Then, when the row broke out, I had a little moist red paint in the palm of my hand. I rushed forward, fell down, clapped my hand to my face, and became a piteous spectacle. It is an old trick."

"That also I could fathom."

"Then they carried me in. She was bound to have me in. What else could she do? And into her sitting-room, which was the very room which I suspected. It lay between that and her bedroom, and I was determined to see which. They laid me on a couch, I motioned for air, they were compelled to open the window, and you had your chance."

"How did that help you?"

"It was all-important. When a woman thinks that her house is on fire, her instinct is at once to rush to the thing which she values most. It is a perfectly overpowering impulse, and I have more than once taken advantage of it. In the case of the Darlington substitution scandal it was of use to me, and also in the Arnsworth Castle business. A married woman grabs at her baby; an unmarried one reaches for her jewel-box. Now it was clear to me that our lady of to-day had nothing in the house more precious to her than what we are in quest of. She would rush to secure it. The alarm of fire was admirably done. The smoke and shouting were enough to shake nerves of steel. She responded beautifully. The photograph is in a recess behind a sliding panel just above the right bell-pull. She was there in an instant, and I caught a glimpse of it as she half-drew it out. When I cried out that it was a false alarm, she replaced it, glanced at the rocket, rushed from the room, and I have not seen her since. I rose, and, making my excuses, escaped from the house. I hesitated whether to attempt to secure the photograph at once; but the coachman had come in, and as he was watching me narrowly it seemed safer to wait. A little over-precipitance may ruin all."

"And now?" I asked.

"Our quest is practically finished. I shall call with the King to-morrow, and with you, if you care to come with us. We will be shown into the sitting-room to wait for the lady; but it is probable that when she comes she may find neither us nor the photograph. It might be a satisfaction to His Majesty to regain it with his own hands."

"And when will you call?"

"At eight in the morning. She will not be up, so that we shall have a clear field. Besides, we must be prompt, for this marriage may mean a complete change in her life and habits. I must wire to the King without delay."

We had reached Baker Street and had stopped at the door. He was searching his pockets for the key when someone passing said:

"Good-night, Mister Sherlock Holmes."

There were several people on the pavement at the time, but the greeting appeared to come from a slim youth in an ulster who had hurried by.

"I've heard that voice before," said Holmes, staring down the dimly lit street. "Now, I wonder who the deuce that could have been."

III

I slept at Baker Street that night, and we were engaged upon our toast and coffee in the morning when the King of Bohemia rushed into the room.

"You have really got it!" he cried, grasping Sherlock Holmes by either shoulder and looking eagerly into his face.

"Not yet."

"But you have hopes?"

"I have hopes."

"Then, come. I am all impatience to be gone."

"We must have a cab."

"No, my brougham is waiting."

"Then that will simplify matters." We descended and started off once more for Briony Lodge.

"Irene Adler is married," remarked Holmes.

"Married! When?"

"Yesterday."

"But to whom?

"To an English lawyer named Norton."

"But she could not love him."

"I am in hopes that she does."

"And why in hopes?"

"Because it would spare your Majesty all fear of future annoyance. If the lady loves her husband, she does not love your Majesty. If she does not love your Majesty, there is no reason why she should interfere with your Majesty's plan."

"It is true. And yet Well! I wish she had been of my own station! What a queen she would have made!" He relapsed into a moody silence, which was not broken until we drew up in Serpentine Avenue.

The door of Briony Lodge was open, and an elderly woman stood upon the steps. She watched us with a sardonic eye as we stepped from the brougham.

"Mr Sherlock Holmes, I believe?" said she.

"I am Mr Holmes," answered my companion, looking at her with a questioning and rather startled gaze.

"Indeed! My mistress told me that you were likely to call. She left this morning with her husband by the 5:15 train from Charing Cross for the Continent."

"What!" Sherlock Holmes staggered back, white with chagrin and surprise. "Do you mean that she has left England?"

"Never to return."

"And the papers?" asked the King hoarsely. "All is lost."

"We shall see." He pushed past the servant and rushed into the drawing-room, followed by the King and myself. The furniture was scattered about in every direction, with dismantled shelves and open drawers, as if the lady had hurriedly ransacked them before her flight. Holmes rushed at the bell-pull, tore back a small sliding shutter, and, plunging in his hand, pulled out a photograph and a letter. The photograph was of Irene Adler herself in evening dress, the letter was superscribed to "Sherlock Holmes, Esq. To be left till called for." My friend tore it open and we all three read it together. It was dated at midnight of the preceding night and ran in this way:

MY DEAR MR SHERLOCK HOLMES:
    You really did it very well. You took me in completely. Until after the alarm of fire, I had not a suspicion. But then, when I found how I had betrayed myself, I began to think. I had been warned against you months ago. I had been told that if the King employed an agent it would certainly be you. And your address had been given me. Yet, with all this, you made me reveal what

you wanted to know. Even after I became suspicious, I found it hard to think evil of such a dear, kind old clergyman. But, you know, I have been trained as an actress myself. Male costume is nothing new to me. I often take advantage of the freedom which it gives. I sent John, the coachman, to watch you, ran upstairs, got into my walking-clothes, as I call them, and came down just as you departed. Well, I followed you to your door, and so made sure that I was really an object of interest to the celebrated Mr Sherlock Holmes. Then I, rather imprudently, wished you good-night, and started for the Temple to see my husband. We both thought the best resource was flight, when pursued by so formidable an antagonist; so you will find the nest empty when you call to-morrow. As to the photograph, your client may rest in peace. I love and am loved by a better man than he. The King may do what he will without hindrance from one whom he has cruelly wronged. I keep it only to safe-guard myself, and to preserve a weapon which will always secure me from any steps which he might take in the future. I leave a photograph which he might care to possess; and I remain, dear Mr Sherlock Holmes,

Very truly yours, Irene Norton, nee ADLER.

"What a woman — oh, what a woman!" cried the King of Bohemia, when we had all three read this epistle. "Did I not tell you how quick and resolute she was? Would she not have made an admirable queen? Is it not a pity that she was not on my level?"

"From what I have seen of the lady she seems indeed to be on a very different level to your Majesty," said Holmes coldly. "I am sorry that I have not been able to bring your Majesty's business to a more successful conclusion."

"On the contrary, my dear sir," cried the King; "nothing could be more successful. I know that her word is inviolate. The photograph is now as safe as if it were in the fire."

"I am glad to hear your Majesty say so."

"I am immensely indebted to you. Pray tell me in what way I can reward you. This ring" He slipped an emerald snake ring from his finger and held it out upon the palm of his hand.

"Your Majesty has something which I should value even more highly," said Holmes.

"You have but to name it."

This photograph!"

The King stared at him in amazement.

"Irene's photograph!" he cried. "Certainly, if you wish it."

"I thank your Majesty. Then there is no more to be done in the matter. I have the honour to wish you a very good-morning." He bowed, and, turning away without observing the hand which the King had stretched out to him, he set off in my company for his chambers.

And that was how a great scandal threatened to affect the kingdom of Bohemia, and how the best plans of Mr Sherlock Holmes were beaten by a woman's wit. He used to make merry over the cleverness of women, but I have not heard him do it of late. And when he speaks of Irene Adler, or when he refers to her photograph, it is always under the honourable title of *the* woman.

At last, thought Kitty, the diversion I need to reach out and steal Missy's swordfish steak.

Lightning Source UK Ltd.
Milton Keynes UK
UKHW012146260521
384429UK00001B/97